Soul of Wood

Jakov Lind

SOUL OF WOOD

Translated from the German by RALPH MANHEIM

📖 HILL AND WANG   *New York*
A division of Farrar, Straus and Giroux

English translation copyright © 1964 by Jakov Lind
All rights reserved
Originally published in German under the title
Eine Seele aus Holz,
copyright © 1962 by Hermann Luchterhand Verlag GmbH
This English translation first published in Great Britain, 1964
First published in the United States of America, 1964
First published by Hill and Wang,
a division of Farrar, Straus and Giroux, 1986
Printed in the United States of America

Library of Congress Cataloging-in-Publication Data
Lind, Jakov.
Soul of wood.
Translation of: Eine Seele aus Holz.
1. Title.
PT2672.I48S413   1986   833'.914   86-7538
ISBN 0-8090-1526-9

To my wife, Faith,
and to my children, Simon and Oona

Contents

Soul of Wood

Those who had no papers entitling them to live lined up to
die. The whole North-west Station was a gigantic waiting-
room. It was a long, long wait, but eventually everyone's
turn came. Those who finally lay in the freight cars thanked
God, and when at last the wheels began to turn and the
engine spewed, hissed, and let out a long whistle, none of the
forty-five had a tear left. Every breath hurt and crying was
torture. Besides, the dead don't cry. The forty-five had died.
Dr and Mrs Barth lay squeezed together, for fifteen years
they hadn't lain so close, and felt neither pain nor cold. They
smelled nothing and saw nothing.

Confused thoughts came to them in their half-sleep. They
saw Anton's open eyes, large and brown and without lashes,
they saw Wohlbrecht's eyes, blue, honest, perhaps a little
watery. Dr Barth murmured, Adonai, and Mrs Barth moved
her lips and seemed to want to say Mama. The train whistle
blew again and again. Anton's eyes grew larger and in the
end they were as big as the Black Sea – as big and mad as
Odessa – as loud as the market, as shiny as the ships on the
sea. The steamers' engines kept pounding out the song:
Razhinkes un mandlen – raisins and almonds will be your
trade. But I became a doctor. Mrs Barth saw the great rabbi
of Chernigev who had taught the mute Rivkele to speak. The
doctor and his wife were both from Odessa, and even in
dying they were still in the same street where they had
played together at the age of four. And now they were both

9

on their way back to Odessa. With a detour, to be sure, by way of Vienna, a forty-year detour and a crippled son left behind, they were going home to their parents and relatives who were also long dead.

But they never reached Odessa. In the little Polish town of O3wiecim they were taken off the train by men in uniform and cremated the same day.

Even at night Anton Barth lay with his eyes open, for like the rest of him his eyelids were paralysed. He wore dark glasses. For sixteen years he had been waiting for his head to die too. That was the most he could do for his parents. In that night of March 14th, 1942, he had a strange dream:

Rain is falling. Everything is dripping with blood. People are being washed out of the houses and are drifting through the streets. The corpses become heavy with blood and sink. But he stays up. With eyes wide open but without his dark glasses, he drifts through the rain, as though swimming on his back. He isn't swimming, though. He is walking with powerful strides. In his right hand a book, his favourite book, in his left the keys to the apartment. Both clutched fast. He is on his way home. He, the paralytic, is walking, while all the people from his street and the neighbouring streets float past him dead, and sink. He sees himself putting the key in the door, he hears someone calling, he doesn't know from where. He doesn't understand the words – there is a call from somewhere, loud as a drum. Then he wakes up.

He wanted to cry but he couldn't, even a single tear gave him maddening pains in the eyes. For some reason Anton had the idea that similar rain had poured down on the day he was born. I was born in a blood-bath, a deluge of blood. But I didn't drown in it. Maybe that's where my sickness came from?

His father lectured to him by the hour, but he couldn't ask

him any questions. His vocabulary was too small. He understood no better the prayers and quotations Rabbi Weiss chanted to him. How will he ever tell anyone about this dream of blood? The dream spoiled his appetite. At about nine o'clock Anton heard Hermann Wohlbrecht's wooden leg clattering on the stairs. The keys made a tremendous noise. He felt that the apartment was empty, emptier than on the Day of Atonement when his parents went to early services. Not a muscle moved in Wohlbrecht's wrinkled face. He set down the breakfast on the table beside the bed and began to feed his patient. He was very quiet today. Wohlbrecht had already wiped Anton's mouth and cleared away the dishes; he was picking up the tray when Anton let out the word 'Mama'. Wohlbrecht studied young Barth, put down the tray, and began to talk, first slowly, then faster and faster, as though he couldn't get it over with fast enough: Left today. No choice. That's right, no choice. Compulsory notice. Or they'd end up in concentration camp. Sure, you don't get it. Neither do I. But that's how it is. Bad lot, the Nazis – you don't fool with them. Your mother and father left me the keys. The apartment is mine now. They made me a present of it so those bastards wouldn't get their hands on it – that was smart of them. Yes, that's how it is under Adolf, the gangster. But I'll keep my promise. You bet I will. I'll spend every single penny on you. But I'll have to sell. Too bad. It isn't much money anyway. First you'll come down to my place in the cellar, you'll spend the night there, and tomorrow I'll take you to a safe place. Not in the city. It's not safe. We'll go to the country. The real country. Where it's green. It'll be like a holiday. Yes, to the mountains. It's beautiful up there. Good air. It's suffocating in the city. Anyway, it's no good for you. They'll put you in the gas wagon one-two-three. Yes, that's how it is under Adolf, they don't think twice, not with cripples, much less with Jewish cripples. Nothing we can do about it. So the quicker the better. I'll take care of the packing. Just food, nothing else. Wohlbrecht has thought of everything. I wasn't born yesterday. Tonight you'll sleep downstairs in my place. And tomorrow bright and early, bugle call, and off we go. Yes, my boy (Wohlbrecht clicked his heel against his wooden leg and saluted), an old soldier knows how these things are done – I know a thing or two, believe you me, I know those damn Nazis inside out. Take the train? I should say not, we're not that dumb, I've got a better idea (Wohlbrecht whispered): Hay! What do you say to that? Surprised? An old soldier knows the ropes. Who's going to look for a cripple in a load of hay? Am I right? Ha, ha. Don't make me laugh. I know what I'm doing. The hay is for the deer – taking it out to the forest, without it the critters'll die on us, so don't make no trouble, Sergeant. Yeah, that's the way to talk to those bums. Friendly but firm. For the deer, ha, ha, ha, first-class hay with a crippled Jew in it. Ha, ha, what do you say? Not bad, eh?

No, Anton screamed. That was all he could get out.

Wohlbrecht picked up the tray and said as he was turning to go: A hay wagon is better than a gas wagon? Or ain't it? Your late parents – I guess it's safe to call them that – they left it all to me, so don't you give me any trouble, see? Balancing the tray like a practised waiter, Wohlbrecht left the room and slammed the door behind him. With his teeth Anton moved his favourite book to the reading stand and his eyes read:

By day gaunt invalids carry my thoughts from daredevil schemes to broad, prancing, invincible certainty towards evening.

Earthquake. The plague eats away my pale face, a silent voice speaks silent signs which only madmen interpret and bear with them unsaid and unforgotten, but at night . . .

He could read no further, the dream came back to him and he was afraid of Wohlbrecht.

The big crate marked Caution Do Not Drop – Fragile – was carried to the waiting cab by Wohlbrecht and the janitor's wife. It wasn't heavy and it didn't tinkle. They had simply folded Anton Barth in two. Wedged in between the preserved fruit (guaranteed nutritious), the cans of sardines and the loaves of bread – the salt was an afterthought, they had just poured it in his pockets – he couldn't move. An air hole had been sawn out under each of the handles. The cab driver didn't like the looks of the crate. He growled: Cost you at least thirty marks. Don't stand there, Wohlbrecht commanded. Give the lady a hand. You'll wreck my car with your goddam crate. Get a move on, Wohlbrecht shouted. The main thing was not to attract attention. The driver cursed and complained but helped. Three times they tried it, the car door wasn't quite wide enough, though Wohlbrecht had copied the exact measurements out of the Motorist's Handbook, which shows you how books lie, and then finally – whish – it was in. The three wiped their foreheads.

Cost you thirty marks. Get off it, you've got your nerve. Can't you see I'm a war invalid? You'd take money out of an orphan's mouth. Come on, let's go – Nutschliggasse 30.

Wohlbrecht balanced one corner of the crate on his knee – the young gentleman wasn't really very heavy – he needn't have taken the preserves, I can't very well open a year's supply in advance, and he sure can't get the jars open by himself, but I owe it to the Frau Doktor, a promise is a promise, Christ, I let myself in for something! His wooden leg ached. Thirty marks is a lot of money, and all thrown out of the window, in a week he'll be dead anyway, I should have delivered him straight to the hospital, they do it free of charge nowadays, a cripple isn't fit to live, least of all in wartime, 'unproductive parasite feeding on the body of the nation' – there is a grain of truth in it, sure enough. But a promise is a promise, I'll have to get the apartment painted first and then offer it to Hochrieder right away, with his low party number he can swing it, or they'll confiscate it on me and then where'll I be. The papers are perfectly in order and notarized, they got to watch their step with a war invalid, especially one with two sons at the front, it ought to bring 4,000 schillings (as a matter of principle Wohlbrecht thought only in the prewar currency). Hochrieder had promised him half in advance.

What you got in that crate? shouted the driver into the mirror. Wohlbrecht's first impulse was to tell him to go to hell, but foresight is better than hindsight. If I say dishes, Wohlbrecht reflected, he's the kind to get suspicious and go straight to the police, in this town it's the innocent things that make people suspicious. My mother-in-law cut up in little pieces! The driver grinned. That old cripple is O.K. He decided to come down to twenty-five marks. You killed her first, I hope, said the driver. You think I'm crazy? Wohlbrecht called back. Too much like work. I did it the other way. The driver laughed till his teeth almost fell out of his mouth. I can't ask him for more than twenty. What a character. Live and let live, that was the driver's motto, he was an Austrian from the good old Emperor's days. Rough on the outside, but a heart of gold inside. Here we are, Nutschliggasse, but next time take a hearse.

Get a move on, cried Wohlbrecht. He had no time to lose. With one tug he tumbled the crate out of the car and on to the pavement. Turn it round, Wohlbrecht ordered, the 'Caution Do Not Drop' sign was nowhere to be seen. Wohlbrecht gave the driver twenty marks and shook his hand. Good luck, the driver said, and take care you don't get caught. Wohlbrecht felt uneasy, walls have ears, he always liked to say. Goodbye, he called after the driver.

Heil Hitler, said a youngster, may I be of assistance? Sure, said Wohlbrecht. Put your books down. The Hitler boy helped Wohlbrecht carry the crate into the yard. Good kid, here's ten groschen. He held out a coin. Thank you, said the Hitler boy, clicked his heels and stood at attention. To help the aged, sick and injured (he glanced at Wohlbrecht's wooden leg) is the duty of every Hitler boy. Heil Hitler and many thanks. Then he took the ten-pfennig piece from Wohlbrecht's hand and marched off. Wohlbrecht shook his head and growled: 'Scum.'

When he lifted young Barth out of the crate, he almost fainted; he looked almost like a mother-in-law cut up in little pieces. A jar of preserved cherries had spilled over him, his hands and face were smeared red, and his eyes were lifeless. He's dead. No doubt about that. Barth was trouble enough alive, what was he going to do with his corpse? Fear that the boy might die en route had given him a sleepless night. They'd lock him up on suspicion of murder, and murdering a Jew whose parents had given him an apartment, that was getting political. It can only end with the Gestapo. And they have no pity, not even on war invalids. They won't even have to send me to Dachau – what for? They'll just unbuckle my leg and leave me sitting in the waiting room until I kick off. He wiped the cherry syrup off Anton's face and poked a finger between his lips. His life depended on the cripple's. When Anton woke from his faint and bit his finger, tears of joy came into Wohlbrecht's eyes. Go on and bite, bite away, he whispered tenderly. Then he substituted a bottleneck for his finger and poured in a swallow or two of schnapps. The schnapps revived Anton. He inhaled the cold March wind and moved from one shoulder blade to the other. Wohlbrecht found a wet cloth, knelt beside Anton, whom he had bedded down in the hay by the open barn door, and wiped the last traces of the sticky juice off his body. He found cherries on his neck, under his armpits and even in his stockings. Goddam mess. He put fresh warm underwear on him, three shirts, two sweaters, a pair of thick woollen trousers, two pairs of warm stockings, then a pair of ski socks, and then a pair of soft fleece-lined shoes (no good to walk in), and stuffed all this in a quilted raincoat (all just as the Frau Doktor had wanted it). What a mess, said Wohlbrecht, wasn't it, as he stuffed bread and sausage into Barth's mouth. The cold and the fresh air had made Anton hungry. He felt warm and safe in the clean underwear, he was almost happy. The sky above the yard was blue, the place smelled of earth. Anton smiled, showing two rows of sound snow-white teeth, an unexpected island of health that no doctor could account for. Anton was burning for adventure. He looked forward to the woods, the mountains and the wide sky, the peace, the animals (he knew them all from pictures), and most of all to the clear, fresh mountain air. Anton had made an art of breathing. Breathing (not ordinary unconscious inhaling and exhaling) was his happiest occupation. It was his private art, not unlike music (for he used certain rhythms, though there was no melody) and not unlike poetry, because it provoked distinct states of feeling. His breathing was a cross between reason and sensation, a wonderful, indescribable experience. In short, it was the art of a total paralytic.

Mountain air was his instrument, yielding the most wonderful, magical variations.

On his way to his hiding place he would have liked to look at the sky at least. (Properly bedded, he might even have seen the countryside and the villages.) He loved the contours of mountains, trees and houses against the blue, as if they'd been silhouettes cut out with scissors. Certainly no one was

16

going to climb up on the hay, nor would a plane be able to spot him; but he forgave Wohlbrecht. Maybe it's best this way. In a time of insanity desires are dangerous. At about ten o'clock the urine receptacle was buckled on him, then Wohlbrecht put him into his 'masterpiece' – it looked like a coffin but was open at the head and foot – and wrapped him in warm blankets. He wound a muffler round his head and pulled a woollen cap over his ears (every detail had been discussed with the Frau Doktor) and began to nail down the lid. The first layer of hay was already in the wagon. They were waiting for Wohlbrecht's brother-in-law. The bastard's never ahead of time. Hermann Wohlbrecht looked at his watch. Already half-past ten. We'll be starting soon, he said in the direction of Barth, who had fallen asleep behind his dark glasses. The old nag's hoofs could be heard coming down the street and a moment later Alois was in the yard. Alois was under thirty-five, but as an epileptic he was exempted from all military and labour service. He washed his hands, brought up phlegm from deep down (breathing came hard to him), and spat vigorously at the only tree in the yard. It's about time, said Hermann, where did you get to anyway? I got here didn't I? Alois gave his brother-in-law a tired, unfriendly look. Together they lifted the masterpiece into the wagon. So that's what he looks like. Alois pushed up the dark glasses and looked with terror into the open lid-less eyes of his brother-in-law's Jew. Get your paws off him and hitch up the wagon or we'll still be here come Ascension. Vaguely wagging his head, Alois busied himself with the harness. But he couldn't get that face out of his head. It made him a little sick. Unlike Hermann, his brother-in-law, Alois was slim and frail, only his stomach was bloated from drinking, and he had a small Hitler moustache (like most of the men in his native district). He had beautiful blue eyes and long coal-black hair, white hands and thin fingers; only

17

the fingertips showed that he worked with his hands. They looked as if they had been flattened with a mallet. But apparently these imperfections had passed unnoticed – he was known as handsome Alois. While hitching the horse to the shaft, he couldn't take his eyes off the woollen cap and the dark glasses that had slipped down a little over Anton's slightly hooked nose. The head protruding from the coffin reminded him of the Prater, where young ladies were put in open coffins to be sawn in half. Next to Anton's box they stowed a smaller crate. Nailed tight on all sides and padlocked, it contained provisions. The crates were roped together and fastened to hooks on either side of the wagon. Over them they piled hay, not too much and not too little. Just right. Last came the stovepipe. It was stuck into the hay like a snorkel. An air shaft like those in the trenches at Ypres. Wohlbrecht's idea.

Go get your coat and don't forget the hat with the bristles. Get a move on. Alois was a slowcoach. A fellow like that, you're lucky he doesn't throw a fit, Wohlbrecht consoled himself. After ten minutes of impatient waiting Alois came back at last. In his coat and his hat with the chamois beard, munching an apple. Then they drove gee-up out of the gate.

When they were on the open road with the last house behind them and not a living creature for miles except the ravens that darted screaming into the furrows, Alois pulled out a crucifix from under his coat. I'll give it to him. If he feels low, he will learn to pray. He don't need a crucifix, you blockhead . . . Wohlbrecht looked at his epileptic brother-in-law with unconcealed hatred. He's a Jew. That's nothing, Alois argued, it can't do no harm. He took a bottle of schnapps from his coat pocket and raised it to his lips. Don't drink so much, Hermann was getting steadily angrier (how did that jerk ever manage to worm his way in with the Wohlbrechts? Not a word about his fits until two months

18

after the wedding). You got to drive later.

You think he's still alive? Before his eyes Alois saw the motionless head in the woollen cap and dark glasses. If he's alive, and I'm not sure he is, he'll thank God he's got such a nice crucifix. The thought that Barth might die on him made Wohlbrecht's throat contract. Don't talk, shut up, you jumping-jack. His wooden leg (or was it the stump?) was itching like mad today.

My foot's itching, he said, it's going to rain soon.

Rain or shine, dust or soup, sang Alois, who was tight by now, we'll knock the Prussians for a loop. Juchei tralala, juchei tralala. He remembered the song from primary school. Pipe down, said Hermann. (But Alois went right on: Our girls the Prussians want to steal. We'll show 'em how to fight for real. Juchei tralala, juchei tralala.) We're on patrol in enemy territory, back there (he pointed behind him) pure dynamite. If he gets blown up . . . (Alois saw woollen cap and jars, boards and preserves flying high in all directions. As an epileptic he was given to imagining things.) If he gets blown up, Alois completed the sentence, then good night! I'll sock him on the head with the crucifix, that'll make him see stars in broad daylight. That'll show him.

Pipe down, screamed Wohlbrecht. Here come the gendarmes, now you can show what kind of a hero you are. Sure enough, two men in grey uniforms appeared on a motor-cycle with sidecar and blocked the road. One, the bigger one, pushed up his goggles over his forehead, and shouted: Where you going, Pop? Where do you think, the Stefanskogel,* where else? Wohlbrecht lied. The gendarme eyed him with suspicion. And from there? he asked. Why, then we're going on up to the game sanctuary, so the critters don't starve to death.

That's fine. Come on down, the two of you.

* Popular outing spot near Vienna.

On his way down, Wohlbrecht rolled up his trousers to make his wooden leg more conspicuous. Without waiting for further questions he gave his answers: the hay is for the game warden, we've only got to take it up, the rest is none of our business. If we don't get there today we'll be in real trouble. I won't get my receipt, because the man won't wait for us, and if I don't get my receipt, I don't get my money. The deer'll have their hay, but my kids will scream their heads off with hunger. Wohlbrecht interpreted the gendarme's sceptical smile as friendliness. If the kids get nothing to eat they won't go to school and if they don't go to school I'm in trouble with the police. But you're the police, so how about letting us go now and you won't have to arrest us later. This man next to me, get that dumb look off your face, Alois – he always has that dumb look before a fit comes on – he's my brother-in-law. A certified epileptic. I'm a war invalid. Seventy-five per cent disabled. But you can't get along on the pension, not now with everything so high. That's why I always got to make a little extra. Who'd have dreamed such a thing back in '14 when I enlisted, the first in my class? The gendarme listened with folded arms, sucking his teeth because you are not allowed to use toothpicks on duty.

You haven't got a pig there under the hay, have you?

We haven't got a pig, Inspector.

Wohlbrecht's stump was twitching fiercely, it ran right down his wooden leg all the way to the rubber. The signal of fear.

The jig's up, Wohlbrecht, he said to himself. Sooner or later, it's got to happen to you. Everybody, my friend, can't live through two wars. After all, you're not a hippopotamus. He waited for the command: Fire! And saw himself blind-folded, shot through the heart, falling to the ground.

Should I first shout Long Live Austria? it flashed through his head. Then at least I won't have died for nothing. Or should I shout: Austria will be free again! like they do in London? Too long, they'll start shooting and nobody'll hear me. I'm dying, Wohlbrecht called out aloud. Alois looked at him in terror. You haven't got a sow under that hay? repeated the gendarme and spat out on the road what he had found in his teeth.

Coal is what we got. And that's the truth.

Three sacks, Alois confirmed.

That'll get you into jail, too. But I'll make an exception because you're a cripple. Now, beat it, get a move on.

The wooden leg stopped twitching, Wohlbrecht got his wits back. Maybe you got a map for me, Inspector? So we don't get lost again. To tell you the truth, the coal is for the Ortsgruppenleiter in Siebenbrunn.

Here's a map. He gave him a brand new one. But listen, friend, don't tell the next patrol about the Ortsgruppenleiter, he was drafted two years ago.

Wohlbrecht couldn't get up on the wagon fast enough.

Gloria, Victoria, with heart and hand for Fatherland, he sang between his teeth.

For Alois the climb up was agony. But once on top he was overcome with gratitude for the cops who had behaved so decently: A most friendly Heil Hitler, gentlemen.

Halt! The leg twitched again. Come down, you. He meant Alois.

Alois crawled down and stood at attention.

What do you mean Heil Hitler? the gendarme raged. With us it's still Heil Austria, you shithead. He gave him a devastating clout on the ear. So you won't forget. If you're going in for sabotage, only the Resistance can help you, Heil Hitler won't get you anywhere. He gave him another clout for the road. O.K., beat it.

The two Austrian partisans on their motor-cycle and sidecar vanished in a cloud of dust.

Wohlbrecht seethed with rage. Hitting a sick man! he shouted at the empty highway. The goddam nerve. Just for that: Heil Hitler, and a double-triple Heil Hitler, and a 'Judas, drop dead' for good measure. Alois held his cheek and cursed his brother-in-law and his Jew. With his last words Wohlbrecht had shown a typically Austrian patriotic pride and a human, superhuman quality that had nothing in common with Alois's mutterings about dirty Jews.

Past Siebenbrunn, on a deserted forest path, they stopped to rest. The hay was piled in such a way that it could be lifted a little. Barth had slept almost all day. He saw that it was getting dark. Here's something for you, said Wohlbrecht, glad that Barth was still alive, and put some pieces of apple and two slices of bread in his mouth. We won't let you starve. Water, stammered Barth, comprehensible only to the initiate. Wohlbrecht set the water bottle to his mouth. Barth drank avidly. The hay dust had made him thirsty. It won't be long now, said Wohlbrecht. In three-quarters of an hour we'll be at the foot. Then you can rest a while. First Alois will carry up the provisions and look round. And if everything is all right up there, I'll take you up on my back. He's an epileptic, if he passes out on the way, we're in trouble. I'll take you up myself even if it breaks my wooden leg. Just a little patience, we'll be there soon! Alois untied the oat bag from the horse and paced back and forth. It was almost dark. The woods looked dangerous, not for a kingdom would he have stayed here more than an hour. But five hundred marks wasn't chicken-feed, he'd get those provisions up if the snow were ten feet deep. Suddenly he realized what they were up to. We're leaving the cripple behind in the woods, he'll die of fright before the night is out. Horrible! On the other hand it was lucky in a way. It certainly wasn't his fault. The Jew belonged to his brother-in-law, what he did with him was his business. Anybody else would have killed him and buried him long ago or turned him over to the Gestapo – but Hermann has always been the honest kind: with him a promise is a promise. Even if he couldn't stand him in every other way, Hermann was honest, he had to admit that. Nobody does a thing like that for a couple of thousand schillings. Downright decent, that's what it was. Hermann's got character, no denying it.

Arrived at the foot of the mountain, they tethered the horse to a tree and began to unload. Barth was removed from the crate and bedded in the hay. After some discussion back and forth Alois had finally strapped the small food crate to his back and started the climb. The trail, according to Hermann, was marked with large stones that should always be on the right side.

Wohlbrecht sat beside young Barth and stared into space. He saw nothing and thought of nothing. The night was cold and the snow had melted in most places. The sky was cloudless and sprinkled with stars and there was a smell of thaw in the air. Apart from the crackling of branches, the falling of pine cones, and the hooting of owls, the world was dead. If I wasn't so stupid and honest, Wohlbrecht pondered, I wouldn't be sitting here. But that's the way I am. He had fixed up the hut for him as best he could, stuffed the holes and cracks to keep out the draught, he had even repaired the leaks in the roof so not a drop would seep in. He would put the preserves on a level with his mouth. There was nothing more he could do. Not right now, at least. That's fate, can't be helped. He hadn't asked for Hitler. Hitler had come all by himself. Hitler or no Hitler, what kind of a life did young Barth have? Even his own parents had prayed for his death, was he who was really a stranger not entitled to wish the same?

Just as he was beginning to look forward to his Turkish

bath, there was Alois again, standing in front of him like a genie out of a bottle. I won't go. I won't go, said Alois, I won't go. He'll die on us up there. Just listening to that wind scares hell out of me. I'd expect that from you, said Wohlbrecht, unperturbed. Let's go, come on, there's no time to waste. You should have thought of that before. I won't go, I can't. I didn't hear those noises when I promised you I would come. Anyway, let's turn him in at the hospital, let somebody else have him on his conscience. I haven't got the nerve. Not for all the tea in China . . .

Wohlbrecht was furious. You don't know what you're talking about. In the hospital – he'd be dead tomorrow. And here? asked Alois. Before the night's out, for sure. See here, said Hermann. Let's talk this thing over sensibly. I'm just going back quick to settle the business with the apartment, I won't be gone long, can't you get that through your head? I'll be right back, and anyway that's how his parents wanted it – I must keep my word, you don't know me, when I make a promise I keep it. Alois just stood there, looking at his shoes. Get going, I tell you, and on the double, Wohlbrecht hissed. What's the matter with you? I can't do it, Hermann, I can't. Keep your 500 schillings, I can't do it. What do you mean, you can't, you jumping-jack, sneaking into other people's families, nobody's asked you if you can or can't, you got to, that's all. My honour is at stake, that's something you never heard of, eh? Please, Hermann, please. Alois leaned against a tree, I can't, I feel weak. You can't feel weak, not now, Wohlbrecht broke in. Pull yourself together, come on. A promise is a promise.

Alois slid slowly to the ground. The crate came to rest with a thud. His hair hung wildly over his face and to keep from falling he propped both hands against the ground. Wohlbrecht was in a rage. Don't you start in, don't you start in now, Christ Almighty . . .

I can't, Alois whimpered, we can't leave him alone, not even for an hour. Wohlbrecht could almost taste his gall. Will you shut up, he whispered loudly and looked – he had forgotten about it in the excitement – furtively at the dark glasses in which the moon and the snow were reflected. Young Barth of course understood every word. When there was silence for a moment, he too could be heard whimpering and panting. Then came a 'no, no' that sounded like a fog-horn. In despair Wohlbrecht hopped around on his wooden leg as if it had been his good one, and finally got stuck in the snow and slush. Everything happens at once, he said to himself. He pulled at the rope on Alois's crate, it was hopeless, the crate was as if glued to the ground and the more he tugged and pulled, muttering curses, the harder it went. Alois clutched the roots of the trees. Will you get going? Wohlbrecht nearly wept with rage. I won't go, Alois screamed. The echo came back like thunder. I can't, he'll die on us. I know what it feels like. The thought that Barth might die before the summit put Wohlbrecht in a panic. Not knowing what he was doing, he hit Alois over the head. A cow at the slaughter couldn't have bellowed louder. Birds darted from the branches, startling Wohlbrecht and Barth. Alois lay on all fours, his arms and legs sprawling. He bellowed louder and louder and the crate wobbled more and more. His face was turned towards the sky, strands of hair covered his eyes. The crate was a square silhouette. A strange, mythical monster.

Wohlbrecht stood pale beside him and bit into his hand-kerchief. Now there was nothing he could do but wait. The rest of the preserves are sure to be smashed and the bread soaked through. Where can I get some more? Alois quieted down but Anton kept on panting. He even seemed to be trying to raise his head. A fine concert. Some mess I've let myself in for, Wohlbrecht kept saying to himself, unable to

25

do anything about it. It looked as if Alois didn't want to be outdone by the Jew. He began to scream again, rolled on the ground and bit into the snow. Wohlbrecht jumped from his good leg to the wooden one and back again and ran in a circle round the two lunatics (they're off their rocker both of them). If they hear it in Eberstal, they'll send a patrol and goodbye.

Actually Eberstal was on the other side of the mountain, but this racket could be heard on the moon if there's anybody there to hear it. After ten minutes of horror, ten years it seemed to Wohlbrecht, Alois calmed down. White spittle stood in the corners of his mouth, he lay on his belly and looked up at Wohlbrecht out of tired eyes. He looks like a dead dog. Some mess. His body was still twitching as in a fever, but otherwise he seemed contented, almost happy. His face began to shine with serene bliss. He even smiled. Are you satisfied now? asked Wohlbrecht. For a moment Wohlbrecht was happy himself, the worst seemed to be over. Then, just to annoy him, Barth began to scream again and Wohlbrecht lost patience. He won't get the better of me, not him. Don't make me laugh. Here I'm trying to rescue him but who's going to rescue me? You've got to keep cool, like in the trenches when you're looking down the enemy's guns. What we need is discipline. Self-control. War is war. Wohlbrecht took a stone and aimed it at Barth's stomach (he would never have laid a hand to him). Actions speak louder than words. And to be sure, the effect was immediate. Instantly Barth fell silent. It was the first physical pain he had felt in all his life. He had never fallen, never bumped himself. This one stone that hadn't even struck, burst like a bomb and set his whole body on fire. He felt a sudden itching and twitching. His finger tips moved. It was a miracle. He had tears in his eyes and they didn't even hurt. They were tears of unspeakable joy.

Wohlbrecht bent down over his baby and spoke calmly,

reasonably: Don't cry, Toni. Stop. I didn't mean to hurt you. But Alois is driving me crazy and if you too . . . Barth stammered something. He was happy. He wanted to show Wohlbrecht his fingers, the way they were dancing up and down. Wohlbrecht, who understood his language, looked, looked at his fingers, but they were as dead as ever. The magic spell was gone. Nothing was left of it but a feverish itching. Barth breathed blissfully. You see, said Wohlbrecht, looking down like a kindly father on his two happy children, you see, that's what the fresh mountain air does for you.

All the trouble and misery of the last few days had slipped away, perhaps he would never have known this joy without it. Barth cried like a child that has found his mother again.

Wohlbrecht unbuckled the crate from Alois and opened it. His worst fears were confirmed. The jars were all smashed, except for two, the bread was soaked and squashed and full of broken glass. He collected the cans of sardines and sauerkraut and carefully removed the splinters of glass from the bread. Got to bury the glass and all. A soldier on patrol leaves no traces. Wohlbrecht looked for a suitable stick: he found three, but the ground was too hard and they broke. There was nothing else to do (where would I be without my pet?), he unbuckled his wooden leg and, balancing on one knee, dug a hole large enough to bury the broken glass and the preserved cherries and plums. Conscientiously he filled in the hole and pounded it smooth, as though burying the disgrace of his origin once and for all. Now he'd have to go up himself. Not one trip but two. Alois was useless. Go ahead and sleep, he grumbled, I'll take it up myself. With the crate on his shoulder he stamped off through the snow and the autumn leaves. Thoroughly exhausted, Alois fell asleep. But Barth was wide awake, listening to the night. Wohlbrecht's footfalls sounded familiar. Ever since he could remember, they had been the refrain of his thoughts. Barth listened to the crackling of the branches, the falling of the pine cones and leaves, the wind whishing in the tree-tops and the hooting of an owl. Somewhere a wolf howled and a fox barked, the moon slipped out of its hiding place to have a look at Barth. All his fears were gone as if by magic. Neither the dark forest nor the solitude frightened him. A happiness he had never known flowed through him like a spring. Quick, clear and exciting. A new life was beginning. An indefinable feeling came over him, as if the sweat that had always run under his skin, over his inner organs, had suddenly dried. Something good is happening to me. But I mustn't see people any more. He heard Alois snoring and hated him: he, Anton Barth, who had never felt hatred. He hated Wohlbrecht too, whom he had adored all his life and who was now in the dead of night breaking his wooden leg on a mountain for his sake. He hated the memory of his parents. Let them stay where they are – he felt a new strength: solitude. It was like having wings; alone and left to his own resources, he glided free like a bird in the sky. As soon as they go, Anton dreamed in a half-sleep, I'll be cured. I have a secret treasure no one knows about and no one will ever see. I don't need anybody. Anybody or anything. Then he fell asleep.

Barth was awakened by a voice: Alois, where are you? Alois had disappeared. Wohlbrecht was afraid. If that bum has run off to Eberstal, it'll bring the gendarmes and that's the end of us. At last he found his brother-in-law snoring in the hay. To forestall any possible nonsense – foresight is better than hindsight – he tied Alois to the wagon without waking him up. Just like the crate. After a short rest and a sip from the schnapps bottle he slung Barth on his back and started off on his second climb. Barth sat with his face turned to the valley, he looked happy and grew happier at each step, while Wohlbrecht felt more and more wretched. The leave-taking

28

sat heavy on his stomach. Hochrieder was no comfort, either. Far from it. But it was important. If I don't attend to it right away it'll be too late. We'll see what comes next. I'll get back no matter what, but first I have to take care of these little details. If I wait another day, the neighbours will break in. Then it's goodbye my beautiful dreams. I won't put the money in the bank, it wouldn't be safe. I'll put it in my wooden leg, then it'll be worth something at last. Just the same, leave-taking is heartbreaking and it's sad to say goodbye. Everything in life is an accident, the rest is fate. Wohlbrecht climbed slowly as if he never wanted to get to the top, the thought of the crime he was going to commit bothered him. But that isn't going to help anybody, neither him nor me. Just make the best of a bad job and take Anton's mind off things. A little good advice for the future can't hurt him either. This isn't the kind of thing that happens every day, so better talk straight from the heart. Give him a tip or two that will come in handy some time. And so Wohlbrecht said to Barth, who was sitting on his neck:

There's two things that count in life, it can't be repeated too often: honesty and hard work. Loafers and crooks have got nothing coming to them. Honest, hard-working people get their rewards. Lazy and dishonest people are in for a rough time. Honesty is a man's most valuable possession. Only man is honest, animals are deceitful. Even a dog is faithful only as long as he gets fed. A man is better than any animal. Animals are nothing but animals because they don't work. People that don't work don't deserve to eat. A man that's honest, sincere, decent and helpful will get his reward some day. Sure, animals may look pretty, but only when they're useful. A cow that don't give milk ain't a cow, a horse that don't work ought to be slaughtered. A hen that don't lay eggs ain't worth keeping. With animals you take your choice, it's easy. You keep the useful ones, you punish the lazy ones by leaving them free. Wild animals are no good at all, because they only do damage and fight among themselves. Men are decent deep down, except Adolf and his gang, they ought to be shot because they're trying to gyp everybody. They all want to get rich and that's what makes them join the party. You think they really hate the Jews? No sir, they just want their loot. And the Aryan Law gives them the excuse they want. An honest man don't need politics, he'll get what's coming to him. (Barth looked forward to getting rid of Wohlbrecht soon, and thought of the deer, rabbits, birds, and foxes whose acquaintance he would soon make.) When I was a kid, Wohlbrecht went on, I once spent a couple of months at my grandmother's. One day there was a knock at the door; it's a soldier pointing a gun at us, it's Good Friday and he says: Hide me quick, grandma, I've deserted. If they catch me, I'll get three years. Give me your gun first, says my grandmother. The soldier was so surprised that the old woman wasn't scared of him that he handed over his gun. That's fine, she said, and now I'll give you a bite to eat. When the soldier had eaten, she gave him a slug of home-made schnapps that almost blew him up the chimney, and then another – and then he fell asleep. Then she went to the police and reported that a deserter was hiding in her place.

They took the deserter away the same afternoon, and for a reward my grandmother was exempted from the dog tax as long as she lived – because she was honest and decent. That's how it is. She wouldn't have done what I done. Of course that wasn't a matter of life and death. I take after her in some ways, but not in others. When I give somebody my word of honour, it's sacred. But not so long ago I had a dream, not a very nice one: I'm in the cellar chopping wood and all of a sudden the door opens and in jumps a wolf. What's a wolf doing in the cellar? I ask like a dope. But he doesn't say a word, he sniffs and pokes in my pockets and grabs me by the throat. And he didn't find a groschen. That dream sure wasn't pretty. But it isn't pretty in the hospital either. When our regiment had to pull back from Ypres, we dug in. And on the third day – we were beginning to enjoy ourselves – we had to move up. Me and my buddies are lying in the trench. And then the death knell rings. Gas. We run like crazy, but you couldn't see with those gas masks, you ought to try it some time. So I'm running and what do I see but my best buddy, stretched out at my feet like in the song, a piece of shrapnel has just gone through his neckbone. I pick him up but he's so heavy he bowls me over and the others think we're dead and run right over us. I couldn't yell with the gas mask on. Then a bombardment starts up, all I can see is smoke, and when I try to get up, a rifle butt hits me and I pass out. When I come to, I'm in the hospital. And who's right next to me? My buddy. He wasn't dead at all, just pretending. Nothing wrong with his neckbone. The Frogs were already in the trench when he carried me out of it. It's hard to believe but my good nature saved my life, though it's not much comfort to me right now, it's getting too damn steep and my back hurts. See what I mean? Wohlbrecht took a short rest. He was exhausted from talking and climbing. He was nearly there, but the last few steps were twice as hard. His belly grew heavier with every step, his good leg was a dead weight, not to mention his wooden one. Wohlbrecht was on the point of collapse, but a man who has lived through Ypres doesn't let any Schafsrücken get him down. Barth had to be entertained, and Wohlbrecht, with gnashing teeth, entertained him: And even suppose the war is over, what good does it do you? Then comes a Third World War and a fourth and fifth, till there's nothing left but plant lice and ticks. That's why I didn't mind the war much, because a war that's on can't break out. Right? But my kind always winds up all right, even if I had to turn into a plant louse.

31

And you'll wind up all right too, Toni, take my word for it. When the war is over, we'll go and see an uncle of my mother's, quick before the third one breaks out, he lives in our village. Yes, he's still there. He's not a celebrity, so nobody knows about him, but believe me, he knows a thing or two. I never mentioned him because your father was a doctor and I didn't want to hurt his feelings; but my mother's uncle, you'll be amazed, his cures never fail. He's a magician. After the war your father can buy another car, or they'll give him one on account of all he's been through, and then, oh boy, we'll take a nice trip, a real nice trip.

My sister can come along with us, and Alois, and my daughter-in-law too, for all I care, and the grandchildren, and even my boys. We'll make two trips if we have to. We'll get there in the afternoon. In our village there's wine like no place else in the world, I'm not making this up. My mother's uncle will be ready. He'll be waiting for us.

When we come to get you that night, you'll come running out to meet us. That'll be the day. We'll throw a party, I don't mind if we invite the whole village, such things don't happen every day, and why shouldn't all of them have some fun? I personally will order the dinner, I know something about it, when I order the *Salzburger Nockerl*, believe me, you've never tasted anything like it. Because I know the ropes.

And next day, that'll be a Sunday, we'll all go to the Prater and take a look at the midgets, the cute little dwarfs, I've been looking forward to them a long time. In wartime the midgets always disappear, same as happened in the first war, but when the war is over, they shoot out of the ground like lilies-of-the-valley, so sweet and pretty, with their tiny little feet and their tiny little hands and their big heads. Like flowers they look. Yes, that'll be the day. You'll be surprised. Do you like midgets?

Wohlbrecht couldn't think of any more just then. Meanwhile they had arrived. It was so pitch-dark that Wohlbrecht couldn't find the hut until he bumped his head against it. Jesus Mary, that's no way to get through a wall. But here we are.

The hut was neat and clean. An army cot, two benches and a table; there was even an iron stove, but no fire in it (who'd keep it going?). With a sigh of relief Wohlbrecht deposited his burden cautiously on the bed. He turned up the wick of the oil lamp. The inside of the hut was cosy – a good hideout for lovers.

Wohlbrecht wrapped Barth in the blanket, undid the urine receptacle, and emptied it outside the door.

Barth was tired and very hungry from the fresh air. Wohlbrecht cut sausage and some bread that he took out of his own pocket, and fed him until he had had enough. Barth looked so contented that Wohlbrecht became suspicious. He sliced a loaf of bread and laid a thick coat of butter on each slice. (That's always nourishing.) Then he opened two cans of sardines and put them on the bench, and next to them a jar of cherries, the last, and a can of sauerkraut (for when he was really hungry). He moved the bench close to the bed. He watched Barth the whole time. Barth still seemed to be smiling. He didn't like that smile. You don't smile in a situation like this. It's indecent. May I have your glasses? And he took the glasses from Barth's eyes. You don't need them in here and my eyes hurt from the snow. He put on the dark glasses. Now he could see Barth's eyes but Barth couldn't see his. He didn't like that look in Barth's eyes one bit. He looked downright happy. Wohlbrecht's stump turned cold. He couldn't leave just like this, without a few words of farewell. But at the moment nothing occurred to him. Outside it was growing light. In the silence a monotonous buzzing could be heard. Planes flying home, he said, but they haven't accomplished a damn thing, except maybe killed a few people and blown up a few houses. Planes are no use in a war. War is in the blood, not in houses. The fewer limbs a man has, the less blood he has and the less he gets out of war. You and me and Alois, we'll always belong together. We're a blood brotherhood. The brotherhood of the sick, the crippled and paralysed. Some day we'll run the world. Health is a menace, what does it lead to? Lunacy and crime. But we shall inherit the earth. Someone like me with a foot missing can get to be a cabinet minister, someone with two feet and a hand missing can become a prime minister, but someone with everything paralysed like you will be king. That's sure to be true. You'll be king because you've only got a head and nothing else. Be a good boy now. With the best of intentions, he could think of no more consolation.

Through the glasses, though they were dark and he wasn't used to them, he could see Barth's smile and the white of his teeth. He felt more and more uneasy. But now I have to go, he said loudly and firmly, and without turning round he went out of the door.

The bomber squadrons were still passing overhead. It was daylight. They glittered in the sun like silver birds, then they changed colour, turned black, and covered the red disc. The way they fly around, the little angels. Wohlbrecht tried his new glasses against the sun. Dangerous little things, but beautiful too.

He felt the crucifix, it was still in his pocket, but he didn't dare to go back.

They had stopped to rest by the roadside between Burgdorf and Burgfeld. They lay in the hay and it was noon. A hot day. They ate with zest and drank themselves happy because they had lived through the night.

From schnapps and fatigue Wohlbrecht fell asleep. Alois

didn't mind. When he felt like talking, he didn't need any listeners. But he made a try, because he really liked it better that way. Hermann, don't sleep, I want to tell you something. Excuses, grumbled Hermann in his sleep. Alois didn't insist and went on by himself. He had taken off one sock and seemed to be looking for something:

When the war is over, I'm going to Transylvania, that's a part of Rumania. I forget the name of the town, but a friend of mine lives there, Karl, you know Karl, he told me about him, this Professor Antonelu. He's no quack, he's a real doctor, he knows his stuff. And he's going to cure me. Antonelu studied with Professor Mückenpelz. Remember that name. But Mückenpelz is retired and lives in Bonn or Berlin, some place like that, he's given up his practice. That's a shame, but it doesn't matter. Because Antonelu studied with him. His last student. Which means he knows what he's doing. They say he does it with saltpetre. How, I don't know. He makes you inhale it and exhale it, but not too much and not too little. Trip to Transylvania can't cost much. It's only a stone's throw. Saltpetre is good for the nerves and the falling sickness comes from the nerves. I know that much. It comes from excitement. You get so excited you fall down. Worry does it too. And being scared.

But the saltpetre quiets your fears and, Karl says, you feel better after the very first treatment, after the second and third the fits don't last so long, and after the twelfth, Karl says, you're cured. The whole thing costs maybe a thousand schillings. That won't be any money after the war. Because once the war is over, once we've lost it for good, we'll get to be rich here. The Yanks will be so terrified of the Russians they'll throw money at us to make us scared of the Russians too. The money will be lying around in the streets in Vienna, you'll see. A thousand schillings isn't much now, but later on it'll be chicken-feed. Once I'm cured, your sister'll come back too. Want to bet? Because I won't have no more fits then and we'll have children. It was hard before but it'll be all right after. You'll be surprised. When we have children we'll get along the way we used to, but no better, when . . .

The loud engine sounds woke up Wohlbrecht.

Jumping Jesus, he cried, they'll fly right up my ass. A burst of machine-gun fire beat down like rain on the tin roof, and by the time Wohlbrecht cried 'Cover!' Alois was dead. Hit right in the back of the head. The blood gushed like a geyser. Alois, Alois, Wohlbrecht yelled, thinking he was still asleep. Alois, where'd it get you? Alois didn't move. Alois, don't pretend, say something. Alois said nothing. It was so still he could hear a beetle scratching in the hay.

Far and wide not a soul was in sight. Even the birds seemed to be asleep. Only the blood kept on flowing. Everything else was dead. It was like the day of the Creation, windless and empty.

How am I going to tell my sister? And the police? Who'll believe me? Half asleep, with cramps in the stomach, Wohlbrecht looked at the blood in the hay. He couldn't believe it, and kept turning back to look at it again and again. The silence made him sick, fear clutched his stomach. Giddy-up, he suddenly shouted like a madman, and as though pursued by swarms of enormous grasshoppers, he drove in a frenzy until he came to the city.

Dripping with sweat, he stopped at the hospital.

Two orderlies – Poles of all things, he couldn't understand a word – threw a sheet over Alois and carried him to the morgue. Like a sleepwalker Wohlbrecht followed them with Alois's coat and hat. They wouldn't let him into the morgue. He stood there, rubbed the water out of his eyes, and stamped his wooden leg. So long, Alois, so long and goodbye, he cried without a sound.

Outside the gate he walked with lowered head, whispering

it's not possible, not possible, started off in the wrong
direction and had to go back again . . . Instead of Barth it
got Alois. It's all the same, he whispered. Two in one day,
two in one day. Two at once.

A little girl followed him. What time is it, please? she
asked. Two at once, can it be? Please, what time is it? The
child asked more loudly.

Now what do they want of me?

What time is it, please? An uncontrollable rage took hold of
him and he gave the child a clout that sent her reeling into the
fence. Ask somebody else, can't you see I'm in a bad mood?

Too frightened to cry, the little girl slunk away.

Wohlbrecht climbed up in the hay and drove over the
bumpy cobblestones to Nutschliggasse. I've buried not one
but two at once. All because I'm good-natured. Who needs
it? he asked the horse and slung the feed bag round his neck.
Then he unhitched him.

Towards noon he was wakened by a thudding and pounding. Someone at the door, trying to get in. In a sweat of fear
Barth shouted something unintelligible, it sounded like a
Tibetan horn. His shout had no effect on the intruder. The
thudding and pounding grew louder, then the door burst
open. In the doorway stood a stag. He looked about, sniffed
the air, then looked at Barth. For three seconds they stared at
each other, each afraid of the other. Barth had no time to
scream. The stag lowered his head and charged the bed like a
bull. The flimsy wooden cot caved in. Then he drew back
and charged again. He flung Barth against the wall. Four
times in quick succession. Barth felt agonizing pain, as if
every fibre in his body had been torn. It would have killed
anyone else, but the exact opposite happened to Barth. In his
fear of the next onslaught, he felt his lids closing and
opening, opening and closing. At the last blow he sat

huddled in the corner, his hands raised to protect his head. When the stag, after tossing over the benches and the table with all the food, went trotting out of the door, Barth stood up and took a few steps. He counted the steps, one, two, three, watched his knees bend, stood still, shook his body and stepped out through the door. He stood outside the hut in the small clearing, turned his head from side to side, and moved around in a circle. He held out his arms and hands, opened and closed his fingers. He made little dance steps, opened and closed his hands, bent his torso in all directions. It soon became too hot for him in his woollen cap, lined raincoat, and three pairs of trousers. But he couldn't stop. A demon had got into him. He danced and spun in a circle, hopped, jumped and sang. He liked the sound of his voice in his ears, he was out of breath. He laughed until the tears came, he cried and kept on going around in circles. After ten minutes he dropped, completely exhausted, and fainted. Some deer, a fox and two squirrels that had watched the mad performance unobserved, now ventured out and sniffed him. A deer licked the salt sweat from his face. The fox scraped and scratched at his leg with one paw, one of the squirrels ran back and forth on top of him. It was high noon. From high overhead, the sun cast bright stripes across the pine-needle floor of the clearing. It now stood directly over Barth. A flitting ray struck his closed eyes. Barth awoke and stood up as if it was the most natural thing in the world. The animals ran away. He looked around him. The door of the hut was still open, he looked in, everything was topsy turvy. Then he believed it at last. It wasn't a dream but a miracle. But whom could he tell? Whom could he tell about it? Wohlbrecht and Alois won't come back. He wouldn't meet any humans up here and he mustn't. Whom could he tell what had happened to him? The deer and the foxes? The cuckoo? He saw a starling hopping about under a tree, looking timidly around. So he told him:

My name is Anton Barth. You don't have to be afraid of me. A miracle just happened to me. I can talk, walk, and use my hands. I'm twenty years old. When I came into the world I was nothing but a head. All my life I couldn't do anything but breathe, now I can talk. I can talk. Incredible. I can talk. See how I can move my fingers. I can bend down too. Barth bent down and picked up a stick. It's so easy. It's natural for other people. But not for me. For me everything is a miracle. I am Anton Barth, totally paralysed, given up by every doctor in the world. Hopeless, they said. I was born with nothing but a head, the rest was useless. The rest of me was a rotten, dried-up nut. I could only scream and stammer. All I had was thoughts and a mouth and eyes. If my parents could see now. But it's too late. They're gone. You should have known my parents. In the last few years trouble made them religious. My father is a doctor. From Odessa. All his life he was an atheist. When the specialist from New York gave me up, they sent for the wonder-working rabbi of Kishinev, he came in an aeroplane. The New York doctor was interested in me as a medical case-history, he wanted my head for his university. The rabbi said to my mother: a child like yours won't have an easy time of it; in other respects he is sound. May the Almighty protect him. Then he went back to Kishinev.

Even at birth I was an embarrassment to everybody, especially my parents. My relatives didn't know whether to congratulate my parents, whether it was the right thing to do; they didn't even insist on having me circumcised. It didn't matter in my case.

I was a sensation in the papers. People made bets about me. Can Barth's head live another twenty-four hours? At first the doctors said four hours at the most. The bets ran to hundreds of thousands of dollars. Some of the bettors were wiped out. But I lived.

When I was five, my neck grew, when I was six, my shoulders, when I was seven, my right and left arm; by the time I was nine I had hands. Barth has hands, the newspapers screamed. They sold standing room outside my windows. But then things happened quickly; within eight months my body, legs and feet grew. On my twelfth birthday they put out special editions in my honour. Just three words: BARTH IS COMPLETE. There was a scandal. Nobody believed my parents and nobody believed the doctors either, and the papers began to insult each other. Nobody was willing to believe I could really be complete.

A certain Hermann Wohlbrecht, a veteran from the first war with a wooden leg, a skilled carpenter who earned a living doing small repairs, became my nurse. He had to look after me day and night. Yes, I was complete, all right, but all there was of me was paralysed. This morning Wohlbrecht went away. I don't think he'll come back.

But I don't need him any more, I'll stay up here, I like it here. Wohlbrecht has done his share. He saved my life.

The starling had long since flown away. Barth didn't mind. He could walk back and forth and he could talk. Nothing else mattered.

Barth began to straighten out the hut. He counted the edibles and put them in the crate. There wasn't much, but if he was careful he could make it last for three or four weeks.

Wohlbrecht stood before the mirror, getting ready. Everything depended on his appointment with Hochrieder. He had brushed his good suit, sewn on two missing horn buttons, and polished his shoe. This was the big day. He was impressed by his masterful face in the mirror. He thrust out his chin and stroked his cheeks. The slightest trace of beard stubble upset him. He found three hairs under his chin and

40

shaved them off. He was pleased with himself. Then he discovered a bump at the hair line, the size of a pigeon's egg. The bump has to go. He'd got it last night from bumping into the hut. That bump could give him away. He took a broad, flat knife and pressed. At the same moment he felt the bump in the back of his head. He slapped the back of his head and as if by magic it reappeared on his forehead, though not at the same spot, but more in the middle. He was getting impatient. He applied the knife again – the bump disappeared again, but this time it cropped up over his right ear. What the hell, said Wohlbrecht. He pressed again with the knife and instantly felt the bump on the nape of his neck. I'll never get rid of it. He was in a bad mood. He hated little blemishes. Bumps, pimples, scratches, scabs upset him. He had no patience with them. It wasn't vanity. No, I'm not vain, he said to himself. But he just couldn't stand such things. A wooden leg is still a leg, but a face with blemishes isn't a face. In a face everything's got to be right. That's how I happen to feel about it. Wohlbrecht pressed down with the knife once again, now the bump was on the top of his head. I guess I'll just have to keep my hat on, he said to himself. He had an uneasy feeling; it's a bad omen. But I'm not asking him for any presents. He ought to thank me. What's 4,000 schillings? After the war it'll be worth twice as much, but after the war maybe it won't be there any longer. Speculation means taking chances. Money is money, even if it's only paper. In a war houses get blown up every day. An air raid could cost him his last remaining hope for a secure old age. Here's what I'll say to Hochrieder. (Wohlbrecht had just found a couple of hairs in his ear and was busy pulling them out. Roots and all, hairs are parasites.) He yelled at himself: the apartment is ideally located. You'll never find a better buy. First the money, then the papers. You're in luck. I could have sold it for twice the price, but I like you. We'll be neighbours after all. I can't stand disagreeable people in the same building. Here's the deed of gift, all signed and sealed by a lawyer. A pure Aryan, naturally. And now the advance. For the other two thousand I'll take your note. Because I trust you. An old party member like you, Herr Hochrieder, wouldn't swindle anybody. To me your note is as good as cash. Six rooms, kitchen, den, and two bathrooms, all furnished. Where would you find anything like it? And it belongs to me. A gift in return for years of faithful service. The owners won't be back, don't worry. Two thousand schillings down and it's yours. The note, too, if you please. Good. Here are the papers. No, thank you, I never touch a drop in the daytime. Oh well, if you insist, your health. Well, good luck. Even the gas bill has been paid in advance. The Jews would call it a *metsiah*. And now, Heil Hitler, Herr Hochrieder.

The speech was just right, Wohlbrecht thought. He put on his hat and his loden coat, pinned on his party badge, and hobbled down the four storeys, greeting everyone he met with a loud 'Heil Hitler' just to get in some practice.

Hochrieder was a man of power. He sat at his desk beneath an enormous picture of Hitler and played with a pencil. He was a tall man with blue eyes and black hair parted in the middle. For his interview with the war veteran he had put on his S.A. uniform. On the left side of his chest gleamed the golden swastika of the old party militant. By trade a beer-hall owner, in his spare time an amateur boxer, he sat there with freshly powdered pink cheeks, for all the world like the Roi Soleil receiving a courtier. He was forty-five, exempted from military service. As Ortsgruppenleiter and owner of twelve houses and four bars, with connections reaching up to the Gauleiter, he was at the zenith of his career. This crippled worm facing him had taken the trouble to make him

42

a present of the deed of a Jew's apartment. The papers were first class, the deed of gift attested and notarized, he estimated the value at 9,000. Surprised that Hochrieder didn't ask him to take off his hat and coat (did I come here to ask for information? No, I came here to do business), Wohlbrecht couldn't squeeze out a word.

Hochrieder put down his pencil and said in a deep voice: So the name is Wohlbrecht? He made a note. Wohlbrecht couldn't bear to have anyone write down his name. He would have liked nothing better than to burn every single piece of paper that had his name on it.

Oh, yes, the apartment. May I see the papers again? Wohlbrecht took them from his inside pocket. Hochrieder glanced through them, leaned back in the chair, and seemed to be studying a particular point closely. He even lit the desk lamp. Wohlbrecht began to feel chilly. After three minutes Hochrieder put the papers aside and spoke: Everything seems to be in order. What are you asking?

Wohlbrecht started right in on his rehearsed speech, whispering it almost word for word:

The apartment is ideally located. You won't find such a buy these days. I could have sold it for twice the price but I like you. Six rooms, kitchen, den, two bathrooms, and all magnificently furnished. Where would you find anything like it? The former owners won't be back, won't worry.

Hochrieder disclosed a thin smile.

About the owners, Herr Wohlbrecht, if I'm not mistaken . . .

Wohlbrecht, breathed Wohlbrecht.

They haven't emigrated, I hope?

No, no, it's all in order. Deported, not emigrated. Nothing to worry about.

Worry? Hochrieder fixed the worm with a stare. So it's all in perfect order. Just one question: Did the Jews have any

43

heirs, successors, children?

Wohlbrecht knew that Hochrieder only asked questions when he knew the answers. One son, he admitted, totally paralysed.

And he is where?

He's gone too.

Where did you say he was?

He's just gone.

I'm asking you for the last time, Herr Wohlbrecht, where is the son?

In the St Veith Insane Asylum, in the section for incurables, that is, he isn't there any more. I delivered him in person.

Hochrieder thought out loud: St Veith Insane Asylum, section for incurables. Good. One hundred per cent Jewish. Very good. That calls for immediate special treatment, does it not?

What do you mean, special treatment? Wohlbrecht was nobody's fool. He'll be liquidated and quick.

Exactly, exactly, said Hochrieder. They call it special treatment. A technical term. So far, so good. Hochrieder reached for his wallet. Wohlbrecht sighed with relief, though he was still sweating. Nobody can get the best of me, he said to himself, and looked up with pride at the enormous Hochrieder. Hochrieder came around the table and stood beside him, so that Wohlbrecht reached exactly up to his navel. Wohlbrecht read: my honour is loyalty. Hell, said Wohlbrecht to himself. What crap. Then a hand pulled him up by the collar, and a deep voice said: Here's a hundred marks for your trouble, Herr Wohlbrecht. Take it. He handed him a hundred-mark note. Because I'm a good sort. You understand. The papers stay here. Until further notice you will not set foot in the apartment. Understand? Until you get permission from me. Is that clear? Because you're a

44

disabled veteran I won't throw you down the stairs the way you deserve.

Wohlbrecht became as small as one of his beloved midgets. But his agony was not yet over.

As for young Barth, Herr Wohlbrecht, let me give you a piece of advice for your own good: You deliver him to St Veith within twenty-four hours or you will feel the full force of the German law. Heil Hitler, Wohlbrecht, and by that I mean Heil Hitler you criminal, you enemy of the people.

Then he slammed the door in his face.

Wohlbrecht stood in the corridor and wanted either to drown or dissolve into thin air. Still, he was glad he made it down the stairs and to the street. He was close to fainting. Me, a criminal? Me, Wohlbrecht, an enemy of the people, me who worked like a goddam fool all my life, a criminal? His heart pounded in his throat. Flames shot up before his eyes. He crumpled the hundred-mark note and threw it in the street. A housewife with a shopping bag and turban picked it up. You've lost something, she said and handed him the money. Lost – that's me, Wohlbrecht muttered. The woman refused to be put off. It's your money, Mister. Keep it, Wohlbrecht heard himself say. I make you a present of it, it's your reward for finding it. Then he ran as fast as he could and ordered a triple schnapps. From that day on, things went downhill with Wohlbrecht.

On his way through the Stadtpark the pebbles caught his attention for the first time. At least a hundred times a year you walk by without noticing, and then all of a sudden you see things you never saw before. It's funny. Very peculiar. In fact, there's something fishy about it. Wohlbrecht picked up a handful of pebbles and sat down on a bench. Summer was coming on and the park was full of all sorts of riffraff. He'd never noticed that, either. Look at all the soldiers (but that's on account of the war, and look at all the children, all orphans?) and all these old people. The benches are full of them. And all these men minus an arm or a leg. What's going on in this park, anyway? And where do all the cops come from? The All Saints procession was over long ago.

He threw the first pebble at a passing policeman. The policeman turned round, he threw another and another. At the next policeman who came by he threw a whole handful. What do you think you're doing? the policeman shouted at him.

Can't you see? Wohlbrecht asked and threw a second handful at the uniform. The people looked. Cut the nonsense, said the policeman. Wohlbrecht refused to be intimidated and threw another handful. The onlookers were delighted at the disturbance. It can't hurt you, said Wohlbrecht, so what are you getting excited about? You're a skeleton, nothing hurts a skeleton. A woman shook her head. He's nuts, she said in a fright, and snatched her child away. The people passed on – even the policeman didn't want to get mixed up with a lunatic. But Wohlbrecht had enjoyed the commotion. He threw a larger stone at the head of the next passer-by (because of that dirty look on his face), and hit him in the eye. The man let out a scream, the policeman turned round and came back. A crowd gathered.

Come along with me, said the policeman.

You skeleton, you miserable skeleton, Wohlbrecht bellowed at him. Go ahead and arrest me but I won't confess anything. I got witnesses. What do you think you're doing? You think I'm crazy? Wohlbrecht was led away by his sleeve, a crowd followed as far as the exit. Several times Wohlbrecht turned and bellowed at the people: You skeletons, you rattlebones. Go on, keep your bones together. Anybody can rattle. I'll show you. And he rattled the change in his pocket. That's how it's done. See. And his hand could

46

be seen moving up and down in his pocket. The impression was misleading. A woman covered her eyes and said 'Filthy pig.' A youngster of maybe seventeen shouted: That's not the way you do it.

I'm telling you for your own good, said the policeman, don't start a riot. Clear out of here quick, or I'll have to run you in.

I'm not starting any riot, I'm just telling the truth. Take it from me. You're nothing but bones, the whole lot of you. You can't fool me. I know a skeleton when I see one. I got one of my own. Up on the mountain. I won't tell you where. But take it from me. I got one, except he's better looking than the whole lot of you. Let me go now, I'm in a hurry. And Wohlbrecht tried to make off.

He ought to be in the Steinhof nuthouse, someone said, and blocked his way. Beat it, cried the policeman. Move along, folks. No rioting.

But the people were already standing several rows deep. Some said in a loud whisper: They've arrested a spy. It's not a spy, said an old woman, it's a Jew. Jew bastard, cried someone standing on tiptoes in the outermost row. Shoot the dirty Jew. You've owned the park long enough, another voice chimed in. Sex-fiend! Jewish swine! Murderer! Jewish swine! The excitement was general, everyone was trying to push forward. Children cried, women screamed. With a roar of: Where's the kike, I'll show him, a soldier pushed forward. Look at this, friends. He tore open the jacket of his uniform, pointed at a scar on his chest and bellowed: A lousy Russian Jew did that with his bayonet. The scar, which had not fully healed, looked like a cancer. Hand him over, I'll finish him off, I'll do it with my left hand. The policeman had to protect Wohlbrecht. Move along, ladies and gentlemen, he's just a poor idiot. Then he ought to be in Steinhof, came an indignant voice. Even when the soldier saw that Wohlbrecht

wasn't a Jew, he didn't calm down. Who ever saw a Jew in
Styrian hunting clothes and a wooden leg? It's not impossible, though. To be on the safe side, he shouted: You lousy
scum, I'm a front-line soldier, see, you dirty slacker. What's
the idea of acting like a Yid? Wohlbrecht looked around
timidly and started to leave. No use fooling with a mob.
Miserable skeletons, he grumbled to himself. But since no
one could understand him, the crowd drifted away. Only the
soldier stood there with his bare torso and a few of the people
stayed to feel his scar.

From the park Wohlbrecht went straight to Praterstrasse
(to quiet his nerves). Her name was Frieda, she was twenty-
two and on the skinny side. Wohlbrecht couldn't abide fat
women. Frieda was always in need of bread and meat
coupons, because she wouldn't sign up for Labour Service.
She didn't work for money, she worked for a pound of bread
or half a pound of pork – she accepted either, but no money.
Wohlbrecht knew Frieda from previous visits, but the girl
had got so thin she was no longer attractive, and after a few
minutes Wohlbrecht was sick of the whole business. Lying
on top of Frieda it was only natural he should think of
skeletons, and instead of calming down, he only grew more
frantic. He longed for a Turkish bath and put his clothes on.
Frieda dressed too, she didn't like Wohlbrecht any more.
She had no use for men that just came to play around. With
her it was all or nothing. Nor could she stand men who came
to her in a bad humour. I'm not getting paid to cheer people
up. I'm not a circus clown, those were her principles.
Cheerful men and men with meat coupons were what she
liked best. Looks and age she didn't care about. She even
took drunks – but only if they were cheerful. What's the
matter with you today? Frieda asked. Has your baby died?

Wohlbrecht didn't like that question. What does she mean
by that? Oh, Toni Barth.

No, said Wohlbrecht. He's just fine. And he eats like a horse. Yes, he's fine. I'm not worried about him, he's got his belly full. Oh yes, Toni is fine. He's coming along fine. They almost caught him, but Wohlbrecht won't let them take his Toni away. When the Gestapo burst in – When? asked Frieda in terror. Oh, the day before yesterday. Ha, you didn't know. Five of them burst in. But do you think they found him? No sir. In Wohlbrecht's place you don't find what you're not supposed to. I know a thing or two, don't kid yourself. I've made him a hiding place in the attic, every time I smell trouble – and I've got a good nose for it – I tote him upstairs. I'm nobody's fool. They can chop off my good left leg before I'd let them take my Toni away. And I wouldn't squeal on him, or sell him, not for anything in the world. They can't bribe me. You know me. I'm just an honest chump. That's the way I am. Oh, if I wanted money I could always sell my skeleton. What skeleton? Frieda asked. Well, my skeleton, said Wohlbrecht, the one I got in the woods. Want me to show you some time? Nothing to be afraid of, baby, it doesn't bite. I could easily sell it to the medical school, it's in a beautiful state of preservation. Absolutely fresh. They'd snap it up in a minute. I got good connections at the medical school, I know a professor, Wohlbrecht whispered. I built him a clothes cupboard in '23. Boy, was he smart, you should have seen his books, all over the place he had books, he even had telephone books in the can, and bones and skulls wherever you looked. What do you do with the bones, I asked the professor once. – I use them to study healthy people, he said. He was a card. I'll bet he's still alive, doctors practically never die, because they doctor themselves, a doctor doesn't need a doctor, everybody knows that. No, I'm sure, I forget his name for the moment, he'll buy my skeleton. And if he doesn't I'll give it to you, give you something to play with.

Go away, cried Frieda, livid with fear. What's the matter with you? You're talking nothing but gibberish. Why don't you get me some meat coupons instead? And try to make a little money on the side.

I don't need money, said Wohlbrecht. Money's not my line. I'm all right. They can't do anything to me. In wartime cripples get along fine. They can't make any regulations for us. My leg is buried in Serbia, damned if I know what's become of it, and my lungs are in France, but they're still good enough to cough with. I've left something lying around all over, and like I told you, in the woods I got my skeleton, not my own, I was just talking, it's Toni's.

Go on, said Frieda.

Sure it's Toni's. He wouldn't eat any more, so he starved to death. Serves him right.

But you just told me Toni was eating so much. You were making me envious. Wouldn't you have a couple of coupons for me?

See here, said Wohlbrecht, for a stiff he looks good and healthy. 'Cause he eats all day. You never saw such an appetite. One of these days he'll eat me too. You'll see. Cut it out, said Frieda, you're so pessimistic today. I don't like boring people. Goodbye.

Alone in the hotel room, Wohlbrecht didn't know what to do with himself. He walked around in circles, but it made him dizzy – he decided to go to the Turkish baths, but put it off till the next day. The Turkish baths won't run away. He had more important things to do. He opened the window. Then he took his hunting knife out of its sheath and began to disembowel all the feather pillows. He poured the contents into the street. Then he smashed the mirror, knocked over the lamps with a chair, tore the legs off the table, which was easy, smashed the bed and bedside table into kindling, and was about to set fire to the whole lot when two men broke

50

down the door, and after a struggle pulled the madman's hands behind his back.

They almost wrenched his arms out of their sockets. Wohlbrecht screamed. He had foam at his mouth, so much foam they could hardly understand him. Let go, let go, you bastards, I got to get to the cabin. Quick, let me go this minute, before it's too late. He can't help it. That's what his parents wanted. That's the way they wanted it. I've got to get him. I'll put him in the attic. Nobody'll find him. He's so quiet, how can anyone find him?

Shut up, you bum, look at the mess you've made. I can't even sue a nut like him. Call that justice?

The hotel owner refused to be appeased until Wohlbrecht, with his hands and feet tied, was taken away in the ambulance.

'Inmates are strictly forbidden to smoke, spit, whistle, sing, make noise, swear, or urinate except in the proper place. Heil Hitler.' For the management of the St Veith Insane Asylum. (Signed) Professor Mückenpelz, Director.

The moment Wohlbrecht read this sign, he sobered up.

Especially the name Mückenpelz gave him a twinge.

Beg leave to report, Herr Professor, shouted Wimper – Dr Wimper – Group B Squad 3 and first Group F reporting for roll-call. Professor Mückenpelz saluted and passed down the line of inmates. That's no way to stand, my friend, he said to an elderly corpulent man: stomach in, chest out, that's better. Thank you. And you, what do you call that, standing there with one hand in your pocket – it's unattractive, don't you agree? All right, then. The inmate he had addressed snapped to attention. Much obliged, said Mückenpelz.

Then he stood facing the men, folded his arms, and delivered his morning sermon: My friends. My topic for today is: the importance of community spirit in our institution. It has come to my attention that one of you, I prefer not to mention any names, I'm not even saying he is a member of your group, has been spreading rumours. The story has been going round – and believe me, it has no foundation whatsoever – that a disproportionate number of patients at St Veith's are dying a violent death. Gentlemen, please, take my word for it that is an untruth, not to say a lie. What we call special treatment in this institution – is just that. The patient is subjected to a special treatment to make him recover more quickly. The treatment is based on a new drug which I myself have introduced here. In only a few hours' time amazing results are registered. Sometimes, in fact, it takes only a few minutes. Most of the patients react splendidly and an average of approximately sixty-two patients a day are treated with the new drug. If you should observe that a friend or acquaintance has not returned to the dormitory that night, it means that your friend may count himself among the fortunates, for he has been discharged from the institution. Because, due to the shortage of space, we send these lucky men home the very same day. That's cause for rejoicing – aren't all of us dying to get back to our loved ones again? – and not cause for worry. Obviously the patient or patients who spread the rumours about violent death are Communist agents. And in the interest of our community, we will make short shrift of them. And so I wish you good morning and a powerful Heil Hitler. Wimper gave the command and as one man the patients shouted: Heil Hitler.

I thank you, said Professor Mückenpelz. You may fall out, if you please.

Wimper took command: Group B, Squad 3 and first group F: Double file. Right face. Forward march. Block leader, take over. To North Barracks. Singing. Get going. The patients sang: When we go marching, out of the gate, Dark-haired girl, stay at home and wait.

Wimper stood at attention. Herr Professor, he said, it's the same thing again. There's only twenty-four of them. How can I meet my daily assignment?

Mückenpelz puffed serenely at an Egyptian-type cigarette, held elegantly between his fingertips. Over the half-lenses of his glasses he cast a smiling look at Wimper, his mortal enemy: In that case you'll make up the deficit from your F group. Good Lord, man, get some sense into you. It's very hard to keep F group up to strength. From a scientific point of view, they are perfectly useless, my dear Wimper, how often do I have to tell you that? Do what you please with them. I give you carte blanche. As long as we have our daily quota of sixty-two.

Herr Professor, Wimper stammered, even if I treat every single member of F group, I won't have enough. They'll last me a week at the very most.

Mückenpelz started to leave for his office. This man Wimper was a calamity, mentally inferior to most of his idiots.

Dr Wimper, I have travel orders for you in my desk drawer. I've only got to sign them. Your Jews do not interest me. Do what you want with them. Now I've got work to do. I believe, he looked at his watch, that someone is waiting for me. Heil Hitler, Wimper. Wimper gnashed his teeth and saluted. My day of revenge will come. For him I'll use a gold needle. Heil Hitler, he said, and hurried after his patients, eager to get his daily assignment over with as quickly as possible.

Wimper sat in his shirtsleeves and held his syringe aloft like a sceptre. Strapped to their wheel-chairs, the patients were rolled past him one by one. Cursing his boss in the most obscene terms, he thrust in the needle with practised hand and pumped fresh country air (as he called it) into the patient's carotid artery.

Dressed as an inmate and flanked by two attendants, Wohl-brecht stood facing the great Mückenpelz. He was determined to keep calm. He spoke quickly but not loudly, pausing after each fourth sentence to see if his words were producing the desired effect. First place, second place, third place. In the first place, I don't belong here. Only Toni belongs here. I just wanted to visit him so I asked the porter. He's not here, he told me. Well, if Toni isn't here, I've got no business here, because it was Hochrieder that wanted Toni so I could get my advance. That's in the first place. In the second place, all I said was the skeleton isn't necessarily here, but it might be, because sometimes you don't have any skeleton left, for instance, when the body's burned, but it's different in the woods because they don't burn anything but charcoal there, so even if you don't rot in the woods you've still got to die, unless you can escape through the air, which if we consider all the possibilities is rather improbable. That's the second place. In the third place, and the third is the most important, because it's the last and I always keep the best for last, I earned it honestly, but I wouldn't have kept it anyway, because I wouldn't have spent it on myself as long as Toni was alive, because I'm an honourable man and there are some things an honourable man can't do. But if he's not alive or if he lives as a skeleton, naturally that's something else again, and then I'd have – it's not so very much money – after a while I'd have bought myself a little stand in the Prater. I've asked around and it would give me a living after the war. The main thing is the investment, once you've got your stand, the rest is easy. Maybe I would have shown stuffed cobras and other kinds of stuffed animals, like frogs and bats, but with that kind of money I couldn't have done anything bigger. A freak show costs a pile of dough, and fat ladies, razor-blade swallowers and ape-men get their pay by

54

the week. That's the surest way to go broke. Of course once I'd got a good start with the stuffed animals, if I managed right, you don't watch your pennies on the dusting, for instance, but you do when it comes to shopping, yes, sure, if I scraped a little pile together over the years, I could still take on a few midgets, because you can't go wrong with midgets. Your food bill is next to nothing, with two yards of cloth you can make three suits, and the public always goes for midgets, because midgets are something the public likes. In the first place they're cute, and in the second place they're little, besides they're people; that comes as a surprise and people like it. But to get back to my first place, Herr Professor, I wish you could give me an intelligence test, then you'll see that I'm here only by accident and that Hochrieder's to blame for the whole business.

Good, said Mückenpelz. Won't you sit down? He gave the attendants to understand that they could wait outside. Wohlbrecht, whose stump or artificial leg, as he called it, was bothering him, was glad to sit.

But the man is perfectly charming, he thought, all those silly prejudices. That name. Where had he heard it? He couldn't remember. Maybe I just thought it up one day, or maybe I dreamt it. You never can tell. Smoke? To be sociable, Wohlbrecht took an Egyptian-type cigarette, though he only cared for cigars. I have sent for you, Wohlbrecht, because I have confidence in you. The moment you opened your mouth I knew you were an intelligent man, and probably – we'll look into it, of course – you don't belong in this institution. I asked the Gestapo for your record, and received it this morning. You have nothing to fear. The secret state police has nothing against you, you don't have a criminal record either. The fact that you were in the service of a Jewish family for twenty years and that this long exposure to non-Aryan influences might have judaified you –

I personally don't give a good goddam about that. As a rule,
I put everybody connected with the Jews – regardless of
whether he's a Jew or non-Jew – into group F, under the
jurisdiction of my colleague Dr Wimper. But I have not put
you in group F, Herr Wohlbrecht, for the simple reason that
I'd hate to do that to you. The Gestapo claims you may have
helped the young son of your Jewish employers to escape.
That too is a matter of utter indifference to me. For all I care
– naturally I'm telling you this in confidence – you did help
him escape. But in the interest of my research work, I'd like
to keep you here a short time under observation, and for that
reason I've put you in the highest class. You've been
assigned to group E. E means interesting cases, my dear
Wohlbrecht, and you are an interesting case. Wohlbrecht
felt really honoured. Group E – my work requires it – enjoys
special privileges, and under certain circumstances you may
even have a pass. Wohlbrecht couldn't believe his ears. But,
my good friend, one good turn deserves another, and this is
what I expect of you: first that you give me your full
confidence, and secondly – this is a request, mind you, not an
order – that you expunge the words skeleton and corpse from
your vocabulary. It makes the other inmates nervous and
leads to rumour-mongering. You will be doing me a big
favour.

   He liked the professor more and more. He was almost as
friendly, if not even friendlier, than the one he had made the
clothes cupboard for in 1923. Thank you, said Wohlbrecht.
It all suits me fine, especially that part about the passes.
Only to tell you the truth, I really do have a rotting corpse in
the woods. But between you and me, Professor, Wohlbrecht
leaned over the table and whispered, I just say hocus-pocus
and the corpse comes to life. I say a quick double hocus-
pocus and he stands up and shakes my hand. If I want to
make him dead again, I do it with a simple wave of the hand.

Like this. And he's dead again. I'm not a magician, but I know a few tricks. But that's just between you and me.

Well said. Mückenpelz took a fresh cigarette. Report to South Barracks at exactly two-thirty. That's where the examinations are held. Nobody ever passes them, but they always turn up interesting material.

It was two in the afternoon and Wimper was through with his day's work. Again the day had cost him thirty-eight Jews and Jewish-contaminated individuals. If it keeps on like this, I can close up shop. He hated that Mückenpelz, that Prussian shithead, like Satan himself. It's an outrage, the things that man does. First that crap about his schedules that nobody can make head or tail of, and now his shitty reports. The bastard.

These lousy Prussians, always finding something to classify, organize, write reports about. Now what scientific purpose do these observations serve? The first sighs, the second giggles, the third cries, the fourth whines. Once the air has gone in, nobody can get it out again. An enemy of the people, a parasite, has got the needle, that's all. There's plenty of people in the world. What difference does it make if this guy was a Trotskyite or a renegade, a Socialist or a Freemason? Giving them the needle is no science. We do it because it's necessary and because it safeguards the German blood. And that's that. To hell with the rest.

Wimper didn't like writing reports. In the first place writing had always been torture for him, and in the second place it was a waste of time. If somebody could at least do the writing for him. Then he could have his reports for all I care. But this way it took up the whole afternoon which he would rather have spent in bed with Erika.

Wimper was a Bavarian, he liked the simple life. He wasn't stuck up about being a doctor. His father was a doctor, so he had become a doctor, but that wasn't anything to brag about. Most people, and not only here in the insane asylum, are so dumb that a title impresses them. Herr Doktor here, Herr Doktor there. That's a lot of bullshit. In Wimper's opinion being a doctor was the same as being a carpenter, it was a living. He'd rather have been a carpenter, a doctor doesn't make beans unless he comes into a juicy inheritance. Science! Serving your fellow men! Professional ethics! Saviours of humanity! A lot of phrases, cooked up by men like Mückenpelz and mouthed by every fool. Was it professional ethics to pump air into people? But you do it just the same. A doctor isn't always a saviour of humanity. Sometimes he saves a life, sometimes he takes one. That's part of the job. Wimper liked it in St Veith, the salary was satisfactory, the honorary membership in the S.S. came in handy, the exemption from military service was a gift of God. (Women are crazy about uniforms, though actually he only wore his when he went to town on a binge). But these reports were driving him mad, the reports and that bureaucratic jackass of a Mückenpelz. Every day he thinks up something new; God knows what it'll be tomorrow.

Wimper put the report in triplicate in his briefcase and started off for the South Barracks. Let him have his lousy report, but one of these days I'll throw the whole thing up. I'd like to see his face when I volunteer for the Eastern front. The mere idea gave Wimper the shivers. They didn't even call it the Eastern front any more. They called it a planned withdrawal. Another of Adolf's master plans. That paperhanger is leading us to ruin. First they should have made hash of Moscow, then occupied England, publicly hanged the king, and sent the whole parliament to Dachau. And of course, the national wealth should have gone into munitions, not been piddled away on whores and liquor. An Austrian corporal, trained in Prussian stupidity: that could only lead to disaster. Oh, if we Bavarians had had a real big shot, not just a lousy pervert like Himmler, it would all have turned out different. To conquer the world you need the Bavarian temperament. Gemütlich, but hard as nails. And all done with refinement!

Wimper strode with firm tread towards the South Barracks, saluted by patients on all sides (he was the most feared man in St Veith and the whole vicinity). Erika was waiting for him at the gate on the far side of the yard. She waved and threw him a kiss. He waved back. He wouldn't kiss her though. That was unhygienic. Never mind, she'll get her surprise this afternoon. We'll have a riot, like Munich in October.

Mückenpelz excused himself to Wohlbrecht who sat facing him at a kind of school desk, and took Wimper's report. He glanced through it.

Fuhrmann Eberhard, age 42, widower: Occupation: clerk; politics: Christian-Socialist; trade unionist. Diagnosis: incurable psychopath, Marxist. Admitted: 22/8/1942. Special treatment. Observation: Fuhrmann had sighed and said criminal.

Wimper, my esteemed colleague. You might have gone into a little more detail in your observations. Yes, Herr Professor, as you wish.

For instance. The sick man gazed at me out of mute eyes and begged me to grant a last wish. He said: I beg your forgiveness, Doctor, for having caused you and the Herr Professor so much work. I realize of course that I have unconsciously sympathized with the Bolsheviks all my life, but I tried to keep it secret in the examination. May my death bring happiness and prosperity to Germany.

Something along these lines, Wimper, that's what I should like to have seen, said Mückenpelz. You mustn't forget, my friend, the purpose of my tests is not to provide you with patients for your treatments. I would do that in any case; the purpose is to register a real change in the patient prior to treatment, thus substantiating our theory concerning sub-human enemies of the people, because otherwise, my good friend, our work would be based on a mere hypothesis, and your patient would actually be right. It would be a downright crime against science if a German neurologist were unable to cure a patient's political hallucinations before subjecting him to the final treatment.

I'm sorry, Herr Professor, but I don't understand those things very well. That was God's truth. If Mückenpelz wanted to be a prize idiot, let him, but to expect such lunacy of him, Wimper, was Prussian megalomania.

Wimper, said Mückenpelz, I must ask you to show more understanding for your work. He turned to Wohlbrecht, who had no idea what it was all about, and apologized. Just one moment more, Herr Wohlbrecht. It may interest you, my esteemed colleague, to learn that the Gauleiter has decided to assign a common orderly as your first assistant. But an orderly can't be entrusted with this, Wimper stammered. I'd love to know why not, anybody can give an injection, he wouldn't even need a course in First Aid.

Yes, of course, but this is special treatment, Herr Professor. Something very special.

My dear Wimper, whom are you trying to fool, yourself or me? Special treatment doesn't mean it has to be administered by young doctors who might be more useful on the Eastern front, it applies to the patient, since you oblige me to mention it.

That's not what I meant, Herr Professor, I just meant that these reports . . . they seem superfluous. He shouldn't have said it, or he should have said it in some other way. Superfluous, Mückenpelz roared, superfluous? Never in all my life have I demanded anything superfluous. The reports will be written as I order you to write them. Have I made

myself clear? Perfectly clear, Herr Professor. May I go now?
Just a minute. This patient, his name is Wohlbrecht, is
assigned to you until further notice as your assistant; as far as
I am concerned, you can use him for sharpening pencils.
There's just one thing you are not to use him for, namely, to
fill out your daily quota. The man will be useful to you. And
now, Heil Hitler. You will be back again at seven. Wimper
saluted and about-faced. The scum, the arrogant bastard.
And now he wants to put a spy on my tail, that's the limit.
Well, he'll be the first to take care of tomorrow. The bastard.
He embraced Erika. Why, you're late again and you look so
angry, she said, taking his arm. What keeps you so busy?
Don't ask, said Wimper. Top secret, let's go up to your place
now, there'll be time to talk afterward.

Every afternoon at precisely 3.15 you will report to me and
let me know if my colleague makes the slightest disparaging
remark about me or my work. Understand? I have ways and
means of finding out whether you're telling me the truth.
Just one lie, Wohlbrecht, and I'll hand you over to the
Gestapo. They'll probably send you back here, but you can't
be sure. And now let's get to work. He took a few sheets of
paper out of a drawer. This test is called the Rorschach,
Wohlbrecht, after the Swiss who invented it. Look at this
sheet very closely and write what you see on this paper.
Every sheet is numbered. From one to ten. You write your
observations in a column from top to bottom. It looks like a
big ink blot. That's exactly what it is. So now you are to write
what you see in addition to ink blots. Are we ready? Start.

Wohlbrecht turned every sheet round ten times and
always saw the same thing.

This is what he wrote: 1. Adolf Hitler; 2. The Reich; 3. The
Ostmark; 4. Vienna; 5. The Prater; 6. Two midgets holding
hands; 7. My best suit; 8. My wooden leg with spikes;

9. Another little midget, but this time in the fat lady's belly;
10. A handle.

Mückenpelz read the answers through and took notes.
That was quick, Wohlbrecht. Didn't you get any other ideas
looking at the pictures? Wohlbrecht may have been crazy,
but he wasn't insane. I can't tell him any cock-and-bull
stories. He'll never believe me. Honesty being the best policy
he said: I won't deny it, I saw Hochrieder in every blot.
That's a little better, my friend, said Mückenpelz. Wohlbrecht congratulated himself on his cleverness and fell into
the spirit of the thing. If you have four aces, you play them
four in a row, that knocks 'em cold. I saw Hochrieder pulling
a knife. Good, Mückenpelz interrupted. I saw him cutting
my throat. Very good, Wohlbrecht. And my own skeleton
without a wooden leg. Marvellous. Mückenpelz had jumped
up with enthusiasm. I congratulate you on your imagination, Wohlbrecht. Excellent. It's almost prophetic. You have
confirmed every one of my expectations, Wohlbrecht. Yes,
said Wohlbrecht, flattered. I don't lie, I'm always honest.
That's how I am. I was born that way. Wohlbrecht was
pleased to be getting along so well with the famous man and
would gladly have spent the rest of his life chatting with him.
I'm an honest soul, all my life I've worked my fingers to the
bone. Some people think it's nothing to be minus a leg, the
main thing is they didn't shoot your head off. It's easy to talk.
But it's not so easy to get along without a leg. It's no life.
Always on guard, always worried about falling down. It's
torture. It's agony. It's a nightmare. But I put a good face on
it. I laugh about it. Actually, I don't laugh at all. You can
imagine. It was pretty tough. Day in day out upstairs and
downstairs, emptying the chamberpot, emptying the pee
bottle. Feeding him. Wiping his mouth and everything else.
Making the bed. Reading him stories. Shopping. Taking out
the slop jar. Upstairs, downstairs. And every minute: Her-

mann, the child is calling you. Hermann, the child is bored. Hermann, don't keep telling him those blood-and-thunder stories. The nerve of those people. The way they kept me running. Those . . . those Polish Jews. Me, a disabled war veteran. Call that justice? You can't imagine how I hated that whole mishpochah. Nobody can. Nobody but me. And the hypocrisy. They were ashamed, that's what.

With me it was: The poor child, our unfortunate son. With outsiders it was: God has tried us sorely. But when they were alone, when they thought no one was listening, it was: With God's help he won't live much longer. If they said it once, they said it a thousand times.

You expect me to be sorry for such people when they get shipped to Poland? *How can anybody feel sorry!* It's disgusting. It's intolerable. Then they make me a present of the apartment, on one condition. Naturally. Does a Jew ever give you anything for nothing? Take care of our child and the apartment is yours. What could I do? I was cornered. Like a rabbit.

Certainly, I say. You can count on me. And they can, too. What I did is nobody's damn business. It would have been easy at a time like this, now we are finally settling accounts with that Jew-pack, any hospital would have been glad to take him. It didn't have to be your institution. But I'm a man who keeps his word. And what does it get me? I get fleeced and they lock me up in a bughouse. You've got to fear for your life every day. That's the thanks I get. Some justice.

Wohlbrecht felt relieved when he had it all off his chest. Mückenpelz looked at his patient and said as though in passing: That's a fine case of persecution mania you've got there, my dear Wohlbrecht. Nobody's going to hurt you. Your rabid anti-Semitism has wrecked your nervous system. Pent-up hatred isn't good for you. Your vision is completely distorted. Hauptsturmführer Hochrieder – by the way, he inquired about you this morning – did you a big favour. He could have had you put in prison for embezzling national property. Instead, you're here with us and well treated. Maybe I'll even give you special treatment. It depends entirely on you, my good friend.

Special treatment. Wohlbrecht broke out in a cold sweat. Hochrieder had told him what that was. No, no, he cried in terror. Not me.

That depends entirely on you, as I said, entirely on the observations you bring me about Wimper, remember? You will go to Wimper's at seven o'clock and spend the evening with him. Tomorrow at 3.15 you will report to me. I hope you will have something interesting to tell me. He shook Wohlbrecht's hand. And now go see your block leader and tell him to get in touch with me at once. Goodbye and Heil Hitler, Wohlbrecht. It will soon be time for your next test, and meanwhile consider that you are being put through a very special test. It's your big chance. Your persecution mania is curable. Your rabid anti-Semitism is nothing but anarchism. And that is pure Marxism. You'll see how I'll drive that out of you. Mückenpelz disappeared into his laboratory to examine a batch of sex organs pickled in formaldehyde, before sending them on to his friend Julius, who was a big man in Franconia. Registered Railway Express. Fragile. Top secret. Not to be opened.

Shaken and none too pleased with his appointment as a spy, Wohlbrecht dragged his wooden leg across the yard.

One good turn deserves another, was Wimper's homespun philosophy. Tit for tat. What's good for you is good for me. At ten to seven on the dot Wohlbrecht was waiting outside Wimper's door. Wimper shared his shack with a dentist. Each had his own living-room and bedroom and his own entrance. Ondula, the dentist, a local man, was a colleague, not a friend. Wimper never discussed anything personal with him, just professional matters; besides, he outranked Ondula. They coexisted in their work and after hours, but avoided each other whenever possible. Glad to see that the lights were out at Ondula's, Wimper gave Wohlbrecht a friendly handshake, and said: So you're reporting for duty? Good. Every Faust needs his Famulus. From now on, you're my Wagner.

Wohlbrecht, by your leave, said Wohlbrecht in a humble whisper. It's all right with me. Six of one, half a dozen of the other. Let's drop the titles, Wohlbrecht. I'm just plain Wimper. What do you like to drink?

Wohlbrecht saw a bottle of cognac, a bottle of wine, and a bottle of schnapps (85 per cent pure spirits) on the table and decided in favour of the wine.

So far he liked espionage. Drink wine, hear what you can hear, give an opinion from time to time; 'report' was a Prussian word that didn't have to be taken seriously. The main thing was to keep sober. Wimper hung his jacket on the door and loosened his tie. He liked this dapper young Bavarian. He had an openness, a warmth that were more after his own heart. Besides, Wimper was young, not even thirty, and not famous. In Wohlbrecht's opinion, he was a nice guy. He was also important enough to be worth getting on the right side of. Sit down, Wohlbrecht, for goodness' sake, what are you standing for, this isn't a funeral.

Wohlbrecht sat down. Got to remember every word, mustn't write anything down. You can be a real help to me, said Wimper, and I'll tell you how: You tell me what the professor says about me, especially threats, it's important to me, and I for my part give you my word of honour that I won't give you the needle. I think that's clear enough. O.K.? Well, prosit. Wimper poured himself some of the 85 per cent.

Wohlbrecht's head was in a whirl. Turning spy twice in

one day. Who'd believe it if I told them, and how frank and friendly the guy is. Isn't that something. Each one of them could rub him out without the slightest difficulty, and here they both want to keep him alive. Two life-preservers are better than one, I've just got to play it smart, thought Wohlbrecht. O.K., he said. Wimper poured Wohlbrecht some more wine. As for your work here, I won't be hard on you, because you're a disabled veteran. He liked Wimper more and more. His own son had never been so considerate. In the morning you can clean up, dusting and that kind of thing; when you're done you come in and ask what I need, in the afternoon you help me with the lousy reports for next day. In between you hang around with the professor, let yourself be tested as often as possible, and remember what he says about me. You can have your dinner here. I eat pretty well as a rule. Fried chicken, schnitzel, anything you like. Of course you could get a better meal in any hash-house in Munich, but let's not think about that. And now suppose we have a little heart-to-heart talk.

Have you got a wife? No. Children? Two boys. Both in the Army. I've even got grandchildren. You wouldn't say so to look at me, would you? Trade? I used to be a carpenter, but that was a long time ago.

Are you in the Party?

No, what for?

Right you are.

What do you think of the war? Come on, out with it, you don't have to put it on with me. I wouldn't report anybody. Well?

Not much, said Wohlbrecht.

Wimper poured himself a big slug, gulped it down, and licked the rim of his glass.

In this kind of work you've got to drink, he consoled himself when he began to see stars. Without drinking I
66

couldn't take it. Not much is plenty, said Wimper.

Wohlbrecht, who hadn't felt so good for ages, gestured discreetly in the direction of the cognac bottle. Here today and gone tomorrow. There was nothing like drinking in good company. Prosit. They clinked glasses. Yesterday I was going mad, today I've got two friends. In wartime anything can happen. Wohlbrecht suddenly remembered that his war years had been the best of his life. Mud, hunger, lice – all forgotten. He saw himself and his buddies in the chow line. Even if there was nothing but dried peas, they always found something to laugh about. Civilian life is dismal by comparison. It's every man for himself and God for all of us. Prosit, Kamerad! stammered Wohlbrecht. His tongue was thick and heavy.

I like you a thousand times better than him, oh, go on, you know who I mean. He's trying to provoke me of course, Wimper told himself through his fog, but he's still an idiot. Anybody that gets shipped to St Veith is an idiot. An incurable case. Whether politically or medically, who the hell cares? Anybody that comes through that gate leaves in an urn. Politically or medically, who the hell cares, he said aloud. The main thing is to serve the Reich. A theory without practice is no theory. Of course I don't agree with everything, but will talking get us anywhere? When we say extermination we mean extermination and when we say keeping the blood pure we mean keeping the blood pure. If somebody's got an abscess, you cut it out. Jews and Communists, Freemasons and clergymen, asocial elements and idiots are an abscess. It's got to be lanced.

That's exactly how I feel. I don't give a damn about anybody except Toni and Hochrieder; for him, lancing is too good.

I like you, said Wimper, almost toppling over, let's drink to you and me being pals. They drank to that and kissed each

other on the cheeks. Hey, Wimper, said Wohlbrecht, suf-
fused with happiness. I've got something for you. You can
help me and I can help you. Alois would have done it, but he
is dead now. Alois was a good man.

I don't need any men, Wimper gasped, close to delirium.
We give them the needle. After the war we'll have a hundred
per cent German patent needle, they're working on it
already, pneumatic, automatic, with all the trimmings. No
sterilizing, no changing. Christ, that'll be the day. I'll pick
my own people, Wohlbrecht put in. Cripples, Jews, and
squad leaders, and I'll line them up.

Prost, Hermann, Wimper shouted. My name's Georg.

Prost, Georg! Here's to your patent needle. Say, brother,
what exactly do you mean by giving the needle?

Before Hitler took over, Wimper explained, it was called
by the French name, *'injection'* with a nasal O – like this.

I see, said Wohlbrecht. When I've got them lined up, I
give each one a hundred schillings. At the end of the day we
round them up again. Anybody that doesn't have his hundred schillings because he's lost them or swallowed them,
either way, gets a good kick in the ass. Because dishonesty
must be punished. Then I'll send them to you, the whole
lousy lot of them.

Every one of them gets the needle, Wimper babbled. That
way, they'll stay honest, they won't be led into temptation.
Because they'll all have to keep step with Wimper. – Prosit,
brother.

The dead and the living are good for just one thing,
honesty to the last breath, Wohlbrecht proclaimed as his
chin struck the table.

I'm glad we see eye to eye, Kamerad. Wimper threw his
arm round his new friend's shoulder. We understand each
other, and Muckbug will be the first to get the patent needle
in the ass, because he's a bureaucrat, a crumby Prussian
68

bureaucrat. Any damn fool can make up schedules and diagrams, but only a master can handle a syringe like a scalpel. And that's what I am. It's God's own truth.

> Heil Hitler to you, Mückenprick,
> A needle in your ass I'll stick.
> Heil Hitler, Mückenscum, to you,
> You'll soon be yellow, black and blue.
> We'll get the furnace burning higher
> and shove your carcass in the fire.

Wimper sang with all his might and even did a few little dance steps, but he was so weak from drinking and wrought up with hatred of his mortal enemy that he soon collapsed.

A man after my own heart, said Wohlbrecht aloud. Taking a handful of cigars from the box and what was left of the cognac, he left the house.

He had plenty to report.

Wohlbrecht had the time neither to live nor to die. Every day was an intelligence test. He shuttled back and forth between the two of them, reported whatever came into his head, exaggerated, distorted, omitted a word here and there, and said neither more nor less than what was expected of him. And he passed. At Wimper's table he put on almost seventy pounds, got drunk almost every evening, went to bed, on Georg's orders, with a few of the female inmates, although 'such' things gave him no pleasure. On the whole he felt happy, contented, sheltered. Hunger and cold were rampant in the city, in the city sat Hochrieder, just waiting to kick him downstairs, while out here in St Veith he was taken care of; if I do as well in the old people's home, Wohlbrecht pondered, it will be all right with me.

But it couldn't go on like this for ever because all good

things come to an end. Slowly but surely the war was coming closer, and one fine day all this would be over. Meanwhile there was plenty to do. Day and night the trucks drove in with new patients. They were picked up in the streets, in restaurants and on park benches, the most dangerous were sent to Dachau or Mauthausen, the less serious cases to St Veith. Instead of sixty-two they now had to handle two hundred a day. It was rough at first, but as time went on (won't the Devil eat flies if he has to?) Wohlbrecht got used to the sight of people dying. He wrote the reports without help from his boss. He knew what Mückenpelz wanted, he wasn't that dumb. Mückenpelz wanted to prove that every single one of the asocial elements delivered to him was secretly and unconsciously a Marxist. That was Mückenpelz's theory, and Wohlbrecht, whose charity began at home and whose own skin meant more to him than that of his Marxists, did what he could to keep Mückenpelz happy.

My good friend, Mückenpelz said to him one day, it looks as if we are going to lose the war. That's in the strictest confidence, of course. Wohlbrecht, who neither listened to the radio nor read the paper, was stunned to hear that the end was so near. Come, Herr Professor, he said, we mustn't lose heart. Our German Wehrmacht will settle Ivan's hash. We did it in the first war, we'll do it again. (I've got to cheer him up.)

Wohlbrecht, said Mückenpelz gravely, the Russians have broken through at Budapest and they can be here any minute. Do you know what that means?

You're a scientist, Herr Professor, they can't do anything to you. Yes, of course, said Mückenpelz smoking nervously, of course I'm primarily a scientist, but I'm also a specialist on Marxism.

Well, so much the better. Wohlbrecht couldn't make out what the Chief Idiot, as he had taken to calling him under his pal's influence, was driving at.

I've just had a little idea. Mückenpelz gave him a sharp look over his half-lenses. Wohlbrecht felt very uncomfortable. When you were first brought here there was some talk about a certain young Jew you helped to escape. It just occurred to me in passing that that young man might be useful to us.

That's all history, Herr Professor Mückenpelz; in the first place young Barth was paralysed and couldn't have lived through the war, he was dead the second or third day, I'd swear to that, and in the second place the young man doesn't belong to us, as you put it so politely, he belongs to me. But why all the excitement? Quite a few people have died around here in the last few years, one Jew more or less can't do nobody any good. You don't understand these things, Wohlbrecht. One Jew can help a great deal. To have saved even one individual would be proof positive that we were not guided by feelings of hatred in the performance of our work. Personally, I haven't much to fear, especially in regard to Jews, I left them to Wimper. I know he's saved up a couple of hundred of them, but that, said Mückenpelz with a sly laugh, won't do him a bit of good. Still, you never can tell. Just to be on the safe side, I'd like you to tell me where you hid that Jew. Out with it.

Aw, Herr Professor. Young Barth's been dead for ages, and even if he were alive, he couldn't say a word. He was paralysed and dumb.

Mückenpelz laid a Mauser on the table. Where is he, Wohlbrecht, that's all I'm asking you. In Eberstal, Herr Professor, on the Schafsrücken, on the highest peak, you cross the river and turn off to the right.

Thanks for your kind information. Goodbye and Heil Hitler. Mückenpelz put on his hat and coat and left the room. Wohlbrecht was crushed. The damn Prussian, first he takes my freedom for three years, and now he wants to defile my skeleton.

The guns could already be heard roaring when Wohlbrecht burst into Wimper's office like a hunted beast. A large, powerfully built man lay on the wheel chair in front of Wimper, screaming his lungs out.

Shut up, said Wimper. What's the matter, Hermann? But he couldn't understand a word. The patient and Hermann kept yelling at the same time.

The Russians are here, shouted Hermann. Let's go and pack, quick, quick. They're here? Who said so?

The old man. He's gone. Quick, hurry.

Don't get excited. The Prussians don't shoot that fast.

But the Russians do. Come on, Georg, let's get out of here.

I'll just finish off these few. Let's see, how many do we have left? Only fifteen, they're the last for today anyway. Wait for me in the shack and start packing. The big man shouted still louder while listening to the conversation. The syringe was pumped into him. Move along, on the double, cried Wimper to his assistant. It's high time. Injections suspended until further notice. Keep moving. Fifteen minutes later he was through with his work, washed his hands, and rushed back to his quarters.

Meanwhile Wohlbrecht had finished packing. You can keep the uniform as a souvenir, Hermann, to remind you of better days. Now (the thunder of the guns was rolling over St Veith, as though the storm might break at any moment. You could even hear the tank treads in the distance) let's get into that car quick. Wohlbrecht hobbled along behind Wimper with the bags. He had put on weight and walking came harder than in the old days.

Georg Wimper checked the engine and loaded cans of petrol on to the back seat, meanwhile conversing with his friend Wohlbrecht.

Say, Hermann, be a good fellow and give me the address of that Jew you hid back in '42, you know who I mean?

What Jew? D'you think I'm crazy, he said. The Jew is mine. You've saved up a whole crowd, at least three hundred. Why do you need any more?

They're no good, Hermann. You can stick them up. I've given the needle to about twenty thousand, maybe even twenty-one thousand, I'm not so good at figures, what's three hundred Jews to that? Not much, if you ask me. But a single one, an individual, one you've hidden at the risk of your life, that would carry some weight. Any judge would get confused by that sort of thing. Where does the Jew live? Come on, out with it, don't worry, they won't do anything to you, you were only an assistant and a patient at that.

Where do you say that Jew lives?

Wohlbrecht was pale. Only an assistant, is he out of his mind? The Russians don't ask questions, they just shoot. That's how it was in the First World War too. He could use Barth himself, a dead Jew is better than no alibi at all. Nobody'd believe he was only a patient.

Look here, Hermann, let's not philosophize, I've no time to lose. He raised his pistol to Hermann's chest. In Eberstal, whispered Wohlbrecht, scared witless, on the Schafsrücken, on the highest peak, you cross the river and turn off to the right. Anyway, I'm coming too, I'll show you.

Don't be an ass, said Wimper and pulled Wohlbrecht out of the car, with all this petrol and your weight? The tires would bust. So long, I'll be seeing you. And good luck. Wimper accelerated hard and drove like a madman out of the side gate.

Wohlbrecht felt utterly crushed, as if the car had run right over him.

Tramping by day and spending the nights by the roadside he passed straight through the battle lines. As a cripple in hospital dress, he got through everywhere. That was a help.

No, it's not over yet, but there isn't much left of it either. Nothing lasts for ever. That's how it is. Just when I'm beginning to find out what it's all about, they stop. I've never had any luck. The war didn't do me a bit of good. First I was good-natured so I got screwed, then I got wise and was doing pretty good, and one fine day, basta, finished. I'd rather have the skeleton than nothing, because if they begin to investigate, they'll find out and that can cost me my pension, if not my neck. And if I don't get there quick, I'm finished, they'll grab it. Can't you go any faster?

The two men in the truck looked at him. The one, Gschwandfänger, was almost a giant, the other went by the name of Bischof and called himself a retired corporal. Gschwandfänger, who had the wheel, spat from time to time at the retreating troops and drove like mad to reach the American lines. On the crates and barrels he had written Nitroglycerine, Explosives, Danger, Do Not Touch, and painted skulls and crossbones. And to make even more of an impression he had tied red rags on the front and back of the truck. He couldn't drive any faster, or else he would have attracted attention, and the poor cripple they had picked up because he had been clever enough to wave his wooden leg at them turned out to be not a combat soldier at all, but a nut from the St Veith nuthouse.

Instead of replying, Gschwandfänger spat on the head of a passing infantryman and Bischof farted so loud it was painful. As I was saying (maybe I'd better tell them the whole story, you never can tell, maybe I can get them on my side) I carried him up on my back. I had to go up twice, because Alois had one of his fits. He was killed the next day – God's punishment; I could find the place blindfolded any day. I'll make you a proposition. I've taken a liking to you boys, you've treated me like a brother, giving me a lift and

74

all, so I'll do something for you. One good turn deserves another is my motto. We'll share the skeleton. Well, what do you say? O.K.? Gschwandfänger had to belch, that Hungarian sausage was still heavy on his stomach, and Bischof took a mouthful from the thermos flask, spat against the windshield, and began to wipe it off. He wished he could give this cripple a boot in the ass, throw him out of the car, and punish him by taking his wooden leg away.

He'd look good dancing on one leg. The idea appealed to him so much that he let out another wind – he could do it at will – that made the windows rattle.

Let's get this straight, said Wohlbrecht. You both got at least a year in the camp coming to you, maybe more, because things won't go as smooth as you think. With the Amis you can starve too. And if they feel like it, they'll put you in a camp for two years. But Toni was a Jew before he was a skeleton and I hid him all through the war. It's just a suggestion, but you gotta admit, it can't hurt you and it might do you some good. I'll say you helped me and they'll send you home with a thank you, because America is run by Jews, just like Russia. Everybody knows that.

Lick my ass, said Bischof, and when you're through, shut your trap.

Gschwandfänger was sorry for the nut. Look, he said, we don't give a shit about your Jew. It's people with a bad conscience that need things like that. My conscience is clear. Wohlbrecht broke in, mine is perfectly clear, I was locked up for three years.

Well, we fought against the Russians, see, and in a couple of years the Amis will be fighting the Russians themselves, that's plain, and they'll want us to help them, you can bet your life; they'll beg us to.

You're kidding, cried Wohlbrecht, whose imagination couldn't keep pace. And now do you see why we don't need no Jew, yours or anybody else's. Wehrmacht or Waffen-S.S., it don't make no difference, we've only done our duty and beat the shit out of the Commies and if we hadn't done it for Adolf, we'd have done it for somebody else. It's no disgrace to kill Commies, that's what they're for, it's the people that fought against us that ought to be ashamed.

We'll be in Burgdorf soon, interrupted Bischof, too bad, we'll have to drop you there, 'cause it's left to Eberstal, and we turn off to the right. Am I right, Ferdi?

Right, said Gschwandfänger.

Wohlbrecht grew sad, for suddenly he felt afraid. You can't be sure, but it's quite possible that those two criminals will get together and cut my throat. He didn't doubt for a moment that Wimper and Mückenpelz would steal his skeleton. These two fellows looked pretty husky. Gschwandfänger was a giant, Wimper wouldn't be able to touch him. The three of us could wipe the floor with them without trouble. Where else would he find two guys like that before tomorrow morning, and Waffen-S.S. men at that; all along the road there had been nothing but Air Force, as if the whole Army had been in the Air Force. Opportunities are rare in life and after the war there won't be any at all, and so . . . (transportation is nothing to be sneezed at either) Wohlbrecht made one last try.

Think it over at least, it's not far and I'll give you something extra. As soon as I get the apartment back from Hochrieder, each of you gets a hundred schillings, that's my final offer, because I can't strip myself to the bone. If I'm ever going to get my midgets, I've got to be a little careful with my money. Gschwandfänger stepped on the brake. I might think it over. It all depends, he said. They were at an intersection. Bischof reached out past Wohlbrecht and opened the door. Go shove it up, he said and pushed Wohlbrecht off the running board. Then he slammed the door.

And they let such nitwits live while we was dying like flies.

Don't get excited, Ferdi, said Bischof, next time we'll take over the home front and there won't be anybody left. Want to bet? And they vanished in a cloud of diesel fumes.

When it's a matter of life and death a wooden leg has toes. The Austrian Emperor's soldier had come to life in him, and that means a man with plenty of fight left. I'll do the ten miles and I'll make it up the mountain. That skeleton belongs to me even if it kills me. It's a matter of life and death, he shouted into the gathering dusk. On the path through the beet fields there was no one to hear him, except maybe a field mouse. Eberstal was the end of the world. It had no streets, no light, and only rain water. Just sixty dilapidated buildings, that's all. No army had visited Eberstal within memory of man: there was nothing worth taking or defending. It was a blind alley, in short, the *culo del mondo*. But Wohlbrecht plodded ahead in the direction of Eberstal as if to catch the last remaining boat, a boat that had already weighed anchor. When dusk turned to night, when the cockchafers flew about his ears and he could hardly see his hand before his face, his heroism mounted and with it his dread of the next day. Hares ran across his path, he stepped on a hedgehog. Wohlbrecht, an angel asked him, aren't you afraid? Shit, was his answer. Hermann, the angel asked him, is there any point in it? Toni is mine and nobody else's, said Wohlbrecht. And what if they kill you and pickle you? He'll still be mine because he's all I've got. But Wohlbrecht, Wimper and Mückenpelz and those two soldiers in the truck, they've all got guns, and what have you got? I'm telling you for your own good, said the angel. I shit on Wimper and Mückenpelz and all the soldiers in the world. On war and peace and corpses and even on the

Americans. On my aching leg and even on Hochrieder. Nobody's going to touch my Toni. Even his skeleton belongs to me.

That's a lot of nonsense, said the same voice. He who laughs last laughs longest. Well, I'm laughing, Wohlbrecht tittered. And he laughed so loud that his own voice scared him. His laughter turned to singing. Soldiers' songs he had learned from his boys, they were good to keep time to.

> Tum ta ta tum down Strassburg Street
> We march with banners unfurled,
>   (Boom, boom went the wooden leg,)
> What if my very own brother's forgotten me,
> It's not the end of the world.
>   (Boom, boom.)

My own br . . . the bum. If he holds out his hand, I'll chop it off. I'll clout Mückenpelz from behind. With my fist. He crumples up and doesn't move. I jam my knife in the giant's heart and let him bleed to death. That leaves only one. I'll finish him off somehow. An eye for an eye and a tooth for a tooth. I'll bash his brains in with my wooden leg. Toni's mine.

Have you got him? the Devil heckled.

I carried him up on my back, he'll come down on my back, I'll put his skull under my shirt, it won't fall out, I'll tie the bones together and put them inside the ribs. I won't carry him in my hands, 'cause if I slip something might break. I don't want a single bone to be missing.

Why not? the Devil asked.

Because he belongs to me. Every bit of him. Twenty-three years are half a lifetime. I've got nothing to give away. That's a fact, said the Devil and flew (buzz, buzz like a cockchafer) away. But he fell at his feet, and Wohlbrecht was glad to hear

78

the crackling.

Halt! Who's there? a voice croaked. A robber, he called back. The way he felt he could have wrung the neck of a ghost. But it wasn't a ghost, it was Elfriede Wurmerer, the witch, who was letting her animals out.

The answer was a whirring, miaowing, bleating and screeching. In clusters and pairs they emerged from the bushes. Twenty-four cats, eight birds, and Gertrude the goat. So she's still alive, nothing much changed here. The smell of cat urine followed the animals, and Wohlbrecht was reassured; he wouldn't have recognized her by her voice.

Is that you, Hermann? she asked. I'd have known you anywhere. Nobody thumps like you. They shook hands. Maybe you've put on a little weight; otherwise you haven't changed.

There's only one wooden leg like mine, Wohlbrecht said, glad to have run into her before anybody else. They hadn't seen each other for ten years and all sorts of things had happened in the world.

She could have died, too; then he'd have had to steal a rope. Wohlbrecht was as happy as a child who has found his lost mother in a department store. It's oak wood, he said, slapping his leg – and as faithful as an oak.

Where's the fire? the witch asked.

Wohlbrecht said to himself, better watch my words. Aloud he said: Nowhere, in case you want to know. I happen to have some business to attend to around here.

Just like that in the middle of the night? Here I haven't laid eyes on you in ten years and you come moseying along just like that. It's not so very late, said Wohlbrecht. Maybe ten.

It's eleven. I'm late tonight, 'cause I couldn't sleep. He screamed again yesterday, I haven't shut an eye all week. Come on in, I'll make you some coffee, and you can stay with me.

If you don't mind, I'd be glad to.

All they've left me is the house, she said on the way. The devils. Everything else is gone. But I won't die for them, they won't get rid of me. Nothing was any help. I've lost every lawsuit. Even though I'm supposed to be a witch. If I could only hex the lot of them to hell. But let's not talk about it, it makes me sick.

A pale moon hung over Eberstal. Swathed in mist. The night smelled of linden blossoms and cockchafers. Nothing had changed at her place. You still had to lift the gate to get it open. She had never been willing to invest in a hinge.

Throw money away? What for? And indeed the steel wire served its purpose of fastening the gate to the post. The pump, as though by sheer will-power, still kept its balance on a pile of bricks. Why spend money on mortar? The two rooms, one for sleeping, the other for living and cooking, were also unchanged. Stockings, clasps, clothes, two crystal chandeliers, and a rolled-up scrap of linoleum were still lying there; they even seemed to be in the same places. The coffee pot was still in the wash bowl. As in former days the whole place smelt of dust and lavender water.

The witch aired her house only once a year. At Pentecost. A house ain't a pasture. I got plenty of fresh air. Which was perfectly true.

She poured water from a pitcher into the coffee pot and set it on the fire. When she opened the stove door to put on wood, the fire lit up her face for a moment. If possible, she was even more shrivelled and wrinkled. Her nose had shrunk to a tiny little bone, her cheeks were hollower than ever, but still rouged and powdered, and her lips or what was left of them were smeared with red. She was an honest-to-goodness witch. At first they had called her that out of malice, but now it had finally become true. She didn't frighten him, but her smell was as unbearable as her stories about the eighty years of her life. She always claimed to be older than she was. Actually she couldn't have been more than sixty-five. I couldn't get old if I wanted to. They call you an old witch just the same, said Wohlbrecht. They hate me because I won't give in to them, and I never will. You can tell them that from me, and I won't ever die either. And she launched into her stories about her love affairs, about the gipsy pedlar who had said 'My, how spry you look with your red cheeks and not so much as a wisp of grey hair, and your red lips, as red as rosebuds, you could still get any man in the world,' about the two husbands she had buried, her son who had died, her daughters who had gone away and got married and never been heard from since, about the lawsuits she was always engaged in – Wohlbrecht knew them all by heart.

It was the lawsuits that turned her into a witch. Pretty near the whole valley used to belong to us, now my neighbour's land begins at the back door. This development was news to Wohlbrecht. Aggravation, quarrels, misery, always wanting to be in the right and always being put in the wrong – a weaker woman would have lain down and died. But she didn't want to die, she refused. I won't die until I've got my grandchild. She had demanded a whole raft of grandchildren once, but now her requirements had dwindled to one. A handsome lad, as tall as a tree, strong enough to tear anyone in Eberstal from limb to limb. That's what the newspapers were for. Her daughters had children, no doubt of that. If they didn't care to write, it was all the same to her, but newspapers have birth notices in them. And if she hadn't found what she was looking for in the last thirty years, it meant either that it wasn't there yet (hence more and more newspapers, regardless from where) or that she hadn't read carefully enough. She had missed it. In that case there was only one thing to do: keep all the papers and take another look when she got the chance.

The whole barn was filled with newspapers. She never got around to looking through them again. But some day she'd have time, so not one paper must be thrown away. She reinforced the paper with home-made glue made by boiling bones over an open fire in the yard. The whole neighbourhood stank of glue, and that was one more thing to quarrel over. Collecting newspapers was part of her life – like the cats she raised, or the birds she had found as nestlings and cared for, or the goat that got older and older and gave no more milk, and like her conviction that there was a grandchild somewhere, because an old woman can't grow old without a grandchild, much less die. She used to lend people her newspapers, but she always insisted on having them back, which made for more quarrels with her neighbours (it's only a newspaper, or, you got so many: both remarks threw her into a fury).

Since the war started, no more newspapers had come to the valley. The radio belonged to Bernbauer, her mortal enemy, which gave her two good reasons for not believing a word it said. Consequently she was overcome when Wohlbrecht told her that the war she had read about not so long ago when the Germans marched into Poland, was just about over.

Did we win it at least?

Of course not, said Wohlbrecht, and it's just as well we lost it or it would have gone on another hundred years.

A hundred ain't so much. That happened one time.

It's long enough for me, said Wohlbrecht. Especially in the last three years. They locked me up. For draft-dodging.

Why did you do that?

'Cause I saw what was coming. A lost war ain't for me, d'you think I'm crazy? I knew it was lost three years ago. In the first place our men didn't have enough ammunition, in

82

the second place the government was taking food out of people's mouths and spending it on whores and liquor, and in the third place we didn't have any trains, so the troops didn't have any supplies.

What happened to the trains? Last time I was in Linz back in '37, I saw plenty of 'em with my own eyes.

Yes, in '37. They were still there. Later on the Jews took 'em away.

The Jews? You don't say.

Sure, I saw it myself. They jumped on the trains like wild men and made off with them. They didn't take just one, they took hundreds. The bastards.

Take our trains away, where'd you hear that? asked Elfriede.

Hear it? I don't hear nothing. I saw it. At North-west Station, I saw it with my own eyes. Yeah, the Jews, and they didn't even bring them back. They took them away to Poland. What do you say to that, all the way to Poland!

But Hermann, what for?

And then they burned them.

Burned them?

Of course. That's the Jews for you; and then they had such a bad conscience they threw themselves into the flames of the burning trains.

'A guilty conscience is a restless bedfellow,' said the witch, shaking her head.

Right you are. And that's what I'm here for now. To check. 'Cause I nabbed one of that Jewish gang, trying to make off with a locomotive. He'd have been in a worse fix if the police had caught him. So I sent him up a mountain, to punish him. That's right.

Up a mountain?

Yeah, the Schafsrücken.

Go on, Hermann, I'm not as dumb as all that, you can't

expect me to believe such rubbish.

It's true.

Look here, Hermann. That critter on the mountain, the one that goes running around with the deer, that's no Jew. It's the wild man, everybody knows that, he's been there since my father's time. And that's quite a while ago. He called himself Rudl then and he kept shouting Rudl, Rudl. But this one calls himself Barth.

Barth?

That's what he always shouts when the moon is full, yesterday he did it again, I told you.

Barth? Shouting? Listen, I'm going to peg out.

Wohlbrecht's face turned ashen grey. He screamed deliriously: I knew it all the time. I'll find him alive yet. Without any hocus-pocus.

I knew it all along. That kinda corpse don't stay dead. Skeletons can talk too, why not, they can jump too, like deer. It stands to reason, they die, get up, and die again. They got no sun glasses. I've got them. He drew Barth's dark glasses from his pocket and put them on. No, now he can't see me. I couldn't see him before either. The corpse jumps and shouts Barth. Not Wohlbrecht, Barth. Wohlbrecht is dead. That's me. Not quite yet, but damn near it. Yes, dead as a doornail. I'm a corpse. A dead corpse. Dead as dead can be. He went to the open door and shouted with all his might: Wohlbrecht.

An echo came back, but with a different voice: Barth! Several times it resounded through the valley, loud and clear. Then Wohlbrecht toppled over and the witch had to drag him off to bed.

I'd have believed the part about the paralysed Jew, but that stuff about St Veith is a lot of moonshine. Do you really think I'm so dumb? Or so old?

She was hurt.

84

While he rested she fixed herself up. No man had dropped in for years, even the pedlars and tramps had stayed away since the beginning of the war. Old she was, but she hadn't given up hope. If it could happen in the Old Testament, why couldn't it happen again?

She had put on her best dress, she called it her snow dress because it was off-white, with little bells at the neck, the puffed sleeves and the hem.

She had braided her hair, put on fresh lipstick and rouged her cheeks. She looked like an old whore or a freshly embalmed corpse. Wohlbrecht drank one glass of wine after another and embroidered his stories as if they hadn't been incredible enough to begin with. Sixty-two a day became sixty-two hundred a day. What were a few noughts to him? Wimper's syringe became a stamping machine (the victims were stamped with poison). Wimper's hatred of Mückenpelz became murder (I saw it with my own eyes, he bashed his head in with a chair). Wimper's flight turned to suicide. (Then he pulls out his pistol and before I can say 'Don't do it,' he puts a bullet through his head.)

Then he came to the Rorschach test:

The professor points to a tree and says: What do you see? A tree, I say. Wrong, says he, that's a house. All right, so it's a house. He points to a field and says: Is that a field? Of course, I say, what else would it be? Wrong, he says, it's a forest. Then he points to a hill. That's not a hill, is it? It's a factory, isn't it? Sure, I say, it's a factory because I've learned my lesson. Wrong, he says, it's neither a hill nor a factory. It's a delusion. The truth is you're a revolutionary Marxist, your method of reasoning and your dialectical lies prove that. Imagine that, when I'd been speaking in my best High German. Elfriede Wurmerer didn't believe a word of it. All she wanted was a grandson. If you want the rope, you know how you can get it. Old women don't get children, they get grandchildren right away. Don't be afraid.

I'm a grandfather already, Wohlbrecht protested, utterly worn out by the wine and his anticipation of the next day. He was already in the bedroom.

Do you want that rope or don't you? Elfriede lured him like a mermaid.

He wanted the rope. No rope, no hope, he improvised.

Well, you won't get it, so there. How Elfriede managed that shameless, toothless, seductive smile was her own secret.

Wohlbrecht could have sworn it was in the wine, Spanish fly. That's what it is. Spanish fly. The slut. What a way to catch a poor weak man. With rope and flies. Is that a way to behave?

All my life I've been driven to do things that don't give me any pleasure. What drives me? What's the matter with you, Schnucki? When Wohlbrecht was drunk he called himself Schnucki, one of his wife's pet names for him.

All right, let's have it then, said Wohlbrecht in a tone of command. In God's name. Smiling like a siren (she looked the spitting image of that skinny whore in Praterstrasse) and getting herself ready by the bed (stockings, clothes, apples, a soda-water bottle, an umbrella, and the caged lovebird had to be stowed away underneath), the witch said:

Don't stand there like an ox going to slaughter, or aren't you interested in that rope? Wohlbrecht felt feverish. Goddam bitch. Using me this way. Hell, cried Wohlbrecht, I'm not even afraid of the Kalifati (an enormous Chinese in the Prater standing in the centre of a merry-go-round). Well, if you're not afraid of Kalifati, there's no reason to be afraid of me, I won't eat you.

Wohlbrecht lost all control. The old woman and the wine, the excitement of the last few days and the impending ordeal undermined his will and drove him wild.

Off with it then, he commanded. He meant her dress. The little bells were run up like a curtain. Jesus, Mary and Joseph, what's that?

It's for my rheumatism, Hermann. It's draughty here in the valley. Utterly flabbergasted, Hermann stared at the catskin pants. Take 'em off, take 'em off, he cried. Elfriede removed the catskin. Holy Stephen, cried Hermann, and what's that? Why that's a cat's tail. No, it can't be.

Yes, Hermann, that's what it is. My dear departed Nicholas was so proud of it to his dying day. You know how toms are. I never had the heart to cut it off. Don't let it bother you, Hermann.

All for a length of rope. Despite his queasy feeling Hermann thought he was at the front again, the order was to advance and orders are orders.

Fur pants with a tail – he'd never seen anything like it. Those pants on a midget girl, it flashed through his mind, wouldn't that be a hit? Sure fire. But it's all so humiliating.

He attacked his pleasure as in other days he had attacked his reports. Unpleasant duties must be dispatched with promptness and zeal.

Thank you and God bless you. She put her catskin back on again. The pleasure was all mine (Wohlbrecht was a gentleman), but when do I get my rope? Right away, she said, where's the fire? What's your big hurry to die? Catching a wild man is dangerous. You mark my words. Anyway I'll baptize my grandson in your name. You have my promise. That's the way I am.

He had made up his mind. We'd better wait. Maybe she'll get away at the last moment. If he hadn't climbed a tree as a warning, things might have turned out even worse. They followed him over the new escape route and crossed his bridge one after another. The she-wolf was close at their heels. It wasn't until they reached the clearing that he saw one was missing. Like a king before a battle, Barth went from one to another, telling each one not to be afraid, giving each one a reassuring pat. They were jumpy with fright, dripping with sweat and frothing at the mouth. But Barth was the leader of the herd and they trusted him.

He knew every stone and every hole on the Schafsrücken and he never left them, even at night.

His own life depended on his power to hold the animals in check; by himself he would have died long ago, in the deer herd he had a chance. He wore his hair under his jacket so it wouldn't get in his way when he was running, he filed down his nails against the stones they rubbed their hoofs on. He kept his clothes and shoes in the crate and always went barefoot. He never went back to the hut except to look for the salt that Wohlbrecht had strewn in his pocket many years ago. Salt was his nightmare, the reason for his fits of recurrent melancholy.

Chewing ferns and licking certain stones did not satisfy him. The animals knew nothing else, but he had tasted real salt, and sometimes the memory of salt brought back wild images of a long-forgotten past.

He was just about to settle down when the animals jumped up and sniffed in the direction of the ravine. Suddenly he smelt it too. Blood. Just as suddenly she stood there, ten yards away, frightened, trembling and exhausted. She was close to death, ready to topple over any minute. Her left hindleg hung by the sinews. He had to push back the deer pressing in on him, aroused by the blood. He only wanted to see if there was still a chance to save her. But when he touched her, she collapsed, as though she had escaped from the she-wolf only for this one touch. In a flash the animals had formed a close circle round them.

Go away! Barth cried. Go away! It was too late. He barely
88

managed to save himself by getting out of the circle. Maddened by the blood, they rushed at the dying animal, frothing and fuming like furies, battering at it more and more furiously with their antlers. A few minutes later nothing was left but the head and a patch of hide. The branches round about were hung with entrails. Barth hurled some sticks to drive them away, but the battlefield was empty now and the animals were grazing peacefully beneath the trees as if nothing had happened. He knelt beside her dead open eyes and was spellbound. The eyes stared at him. He heard voices in his ear and suddenly they were standing beside him, larger than life. They looked down at him and were silent. As though to defend himself, Barth picked up the dead doe's head and held out the lifeless eyes towards them.

Say something, say something, he screamed. But his father only shook his head. His mother shook her head too. Say something! Speak to me! I'm afraid!

Suddenly he heard his father's voice plain and clear: No, we don't want him. His mother repeated: No, no, we don't want him.

Numbed by fear and shock, he dropped the head. One of the deer had touched him with its antlers; and with his last strength Barth rose to his feet and broke out of the circle. He ran through the night forest as if pursued by monsters. Higher and higher. He didn't dare turn round until he saw the hut. The animals hadn't followed him. Panting he leaned against a tree, willing to believe that what had happened had been one of his salt dreams.

A cold shiver turned him to ice. Human shadows were moving through the bushes, he heard crackling in the underbrush.

It was no dream, his heart pounded in his throat, and suddenly a voice from far away shouted clearly: Wohlbrecht! Barth! Barth! Barth! he called back. The sound of his own voice gave him just enough strength to reach the hut. Bracing his back against the door, he sat huddled up, staring wide-eyed at the barred windows.

The procession had reached the foot of the mountain. The ceremonial had not changed. Four cats in the lead, then another four, then Gerti the goat, then the rest of the cats, and drawing up the rear, the eight birds. She carried a sick cat in her arms, though ordinarily she wasn't one to spoil them. Wohlbrecht hobbled along beside her, carrying a rope over his shoulder like a mountain climber. If he stamps his right hoof you quickly say two Our Fathers, if he bares his tusks and hisses, down on your knees and say three Hail Marys, but if you see the smoke, it's white and comes out of his nose and ears, close your eyes quick or it'll blind you. I've warned you, but you won't listen. Isn't the salt running out of your pockets? Wohlbrecht felt his coat pockets. The witch had filled them with salt – without salt you won't even get near enough to see him.

And now you'd better get started and be sure to get up there before noon, because at the stroke of noon he can't stand seeing anybody. So goodbye. In God's name.

Wohlbrecht looked at her: Your superstitious nonsense would kill a cow. You Eberstal people are all heathens. But thanks for putting me up and thanks for the rope.

I've got to bring him down. I owe it to his parents. If I don't find him, I'll wait up there until I do. I'm not afraid, that's plain as day.

There was so much fear in his eyes it made him blink. Knock three times and don't forget those newspapers you've got in the crate. That's it.

She made the sign of the cross over him and turned round. Let him bash his mulish skull in. The wild man will eat him to the bone. So old and still such a nut. You don't go fooling around with a wild man, hasn't he done enough damage already? In three years not a right baby born in the village, and four floods and ten people killed each time. And the big horseflies, as big as canaries? And all these years not a single apple but had worms in it? And the ten thousand swallows that fell out of the sky last spring? I suppose that's nothing. Let him break his fool neck. Serve him right. Followed by her retinue, she went back to her house without so much as a look back.

Hocus-pocus, Toni-corpse. Look, I've brought you some salt. He didn't find the corpse, and there was no skeleton to be seen. But he didn't dare go into the hut. Salt, salt, look here. Salt, salt. No answer. He was worn out from the climb – three years in St Veith and seventy pounds had made an old man of him. Feeling weak, he lay down on his belly. Salt, salt. Come on, sweetie, come. He sprinkled salt in front of him. Suddenly he heard something burst out of the hut and saw someone disappear into the woods. Paralysed by terror and exhaustion, he screamed his: Salt, salt, come on, sweetie. Nothing came and nothing stirred. Wohlbrecht fell into a brief cat-nap. While he lay there as if dead, the deer ventured nearer, and even Barth came close. They licked it from his hands and out of his pockets. Wohlbrecht started up and froze. Barth was kneeling beside him, licking the salt from the ground. I'm going to die of fright, was his first thought. Is that you, Toni? he asked. Barth looked at him. A second passed. With his last strength, Wohlbrecht darted out his arm as quick as a snake's tongue and seized Barth by the leg. He held fast, Barth tried to break loose and dragged Wohlbrecht several feet along the ground. But Wohlbrecht was too heavy. In a flash he flung himself on Barth. Barth hissed, growled, screamed, and bit his hand. But Wohlbrecht didn't let go. He clung to Barth with his last remaining strength. When he had caught his breath, he shouted furiously: You sneaky little bastard, play-acting all these years, lying to me, you sneak, did I deserve that? Here's one for you, and another and another. He hammered at him with his fist. With a final effort he trussed him up like a sheep and gagged him with the end of the rope.

Good. Well, now I've got what I need. Barth didn't budge. Wohlbrecht broke out in a sweat. That rascal sure knows how to pretend. He slapped Barth's face several times, and didn't breathe easy until he heard him moan.

He lifted Barth over his shoulder and tried to stand up. Finally he made it. Barth was three times as heavy. The little sneak has put on weight. That's all I needed. He's heavy, Wohlbrecht lamented, I'll never get him down, I'll never make it alone, somebody's got to help me. He could hardly breathe and had to stop at every step. I'll never make it alone.

As though in response to a command, three of them jumped out from behind a clump of bushes. Hands up, shouted the tallest. Wohlbrecht recognized him at once. He was the driver of the day before. The younger one was Georg Wimper, unshaven and almost unrecognizable, and the doddering old man beside him with the half-lenses, the hat, winter overcoat and galoshes was Professor Mückenpelz. The fourth is missing, it ran through Wohlbrecht's head. He dropped Barth like a sack of potatoes.

Herr Barth, said Gschwandfänger to the bundle, you are free. Cut the cords, he ordered Mückenpelz. Mückenpelz took his pocket knife and began to scrape at the rope. Too slowly for Lieutenant Gschwandfänger. With a jerk of his bayonet he freed Barth from his bonds.

We've come to rescue you, said Georg Wimper. Say, you need a little pepping up. Look what the swine's done to you. He'll get what's coming to him, Gschwandfänger proclaimed. Wohlbrecht sat on the ground, holding his wooden leg with both hands. Meanwhile Barth dragged himself painfully to his feet. I'd like to see a deer do that. But they'll stuff me anyway. He could see himself over a bar as in pictures of country inns. Without antlers it's even more impressive.

Anton Barth, said Gschwandfänger in an official tone, where are your papers?

I'm a deer, said Barth.

He can talk, he can talk, Holy Jesus, God in heaven, a miracle, I'm dying, cried Wohlbrecht.

Everything in its proper order, said Gschwandfänger. First let's give him something to eat.

Wimper nudged Mückenpelz, who opened the knapsack. He took out a salami and a quarter loaf of black bread, and handed them to Wimper.

Here, my boy, said Wimper. But Barth refused. Eat! Wimper ordered. People that don't eat get sick. But Barth shook his head in disgust.

You've got to eat, Wimper repeated.

Pull his mouth open if he don't want to. Gschwandfänger had no patience with slowcoaches. Sit down, he ordered Barth, and pressed him down by the shoulders. Open your mouth! But Barth, sickened by the smell of the sausage, refused. They forced his mouth open. Why, there's hay in it, Wimper screamed.

Out with the hay, Gschwandfänger commanded. Wimper reached into Barth's mouth and removed the hay from the teeth. That's not really my job, he thought. Good. And now, eat, man. But they had to hold his nose. Barth managed to get the first slice of salami down, but the bread turned his stomach.

Swine! Gschwandfänger was furious. The bastard's messed up my whole uniform. He wiped himself off with a handful or two of grass.

Lousy Jewish pig, said Wimper helpfully. Instantly Gschwandfänger clouted him over the head. Herr Barth is his name, he roared. Gschwandfänger had a quick temper; he was a professional soldier and couldn't abide subordinates. Let them capitulate as much as they please in Berlin, up here on the mountain there's going to be discipline.

Mückenpelz knelt down beside Barth and spoke softly: Herr Barth, I beg of you, don't make things hard for us. We only want to help you.

Barth lay flat on his back, his head to one side, looking up at the tops of the fir trees that cut like knives into the grey sky. He gave out hoarse cries that sounded like mooing.

Quick, Georg, Gschwandfänger ordered, now he's got his mouth open, pour in some cognac. Wimper poured in cognac. The cognac had a miraculous effect. The first gulp made Barth dizzy, but he sat up. With one hand he wrenched the bottle away from Wimper and set it to his lips. Not so fast, Wimper protested. We haven't got that much. And he took the bottle away.

Barth felt wonderful. He was still making horrible faces, but he stood up.

Prosit! they all cried in unison. He's alive.

They handed the bottle round and even Wohlbrecht had a swallow. Prosit, he cried. His hopes were reviving again. A bird in the hand is worth two in the bush.

I'll make you a proposition, said Wohlbrecht. We'll share Barth. I've never been a piker.

Share? Gschwandfänger burst into a whinny.

What do you mean share? Have you got something to share? You think we're crazy? People share when they have to. I suppose you're going to make us? I'll make you a counterproposal: if you persuade Barth to come with us quietly, because it wouldn't do to use force, and sign a paper

94

saying we brought him up here at the risk of our lives, we'll let you off scot-free.

For a moment Wohlbrecht was too flabbergasted to answer. Am I crazy or am I deaf? Aloud he said: I don't understand a word you're saying.

Mückenpelz wrote it out for him on a piece of paper: 'I, Hermann, Wohlbrecht, solemnly swear that Lieutenant Ferdinand Gschwandfänger, Dr Georg Wimper and Professor Caesar Mückenpelz gave me every possible help in saving Anton Barth, a victim of racial persecution, from the clutches of the Gestapo. Signed.'

Mückenpelz held out the pen. Sign! The tone struck a familiar chord. Wohlbrecht signed. Excellent, said Mückenpelz. And now, gentlemen, perhaps we had better be going.

What are you going to do with him? Wohlbrecht asked. He still couldn't take it all in.

A few weeks' vacation in Eberstal can't hurt us. We'll bide our time. The rest will take care of itself, said Wimper in a tone that was almost friendly.

Barth looked bleary-eyed at Wohlbrecht.

Go on down, Toni, go on down. And kiss the folks at home. Goodbye Toni, goodbye. The apartment will be yours now. You'll think of me once in a while, won't you? I'll be down after a while. But not right away.

Georg held one end of the rope, Barth was tied to the other. When Gschwandfänger, who was in the lead, disappeared behind a tree, Wohlbrecht came to his senses.

It's a crime. It's got to be stopped. They mustn't go on. Not with my Toni. In a few seconds his whole botched life passed before his eyes. He couldn't stand it:

He's mine, mine, he shouted with all his might. Barth is mine. Criminals! Scoundrels! Crooks! Give him back. Gschwandfänger about-faced. The others came goose-stepping after him.

If you keep on shouting, he said calmly, you'll be breaking your promise, and besides they'll hear you all over the valley. Foaming at the mouth, Wohlbrecht bellowed: You can't do it. He's mine. I hid him. Me and nobody else.

Quiet! Wimper ordered. They can hear you in Eberstal. But Wohlbrecht was beyond control: Let him go! This minute! Let him go! I've got to bring him back. I've got to.

Nobody's got to do anything. Except die, like Bischof. Those gangsters didn't ask any questions. They just shot him. I for one thought it over and at the last moment took your advice. So what do you want now?

I owe it to my soul, Wohlbrecht whined.

Stop whining, Gschwandfänger commanded. He thrust one foot forward and held his thumb in his belt. What a dog this cripple is. Nauseating.

He was in an ugly mood and felt like teasing the old man some more.

Where do you keep your soul, you creep? I bet you never had one.

Here, cried Wohlbrecht, here. He pointed to his wooden leg. Is that nothing? Have you no pity?

With one tug Gschwandfänger pulled off the wooden leg and flung it against a tree. No soul here, he said. It was no good anyway. Buckle it on tighter next time. Let's go! They started off again.

Have mercy, Wohlbrecht begged on one knee. I'm human too.

Gschwandfänger turned round quickly and handed Mückenpelz the submachine gun he had hidden under his coat. Shall we have mercy? All right. And to Wohlbrecht he said: We wouldn't do it if we weren't kind-hearted. Go ahead, Mucky, you old shithead.

Mückenpelz aimed the pistol with trembling hands. But

96

he couldn't do anything without a preamble: Wohlbrecht, you're a bad sort, or I couldn't do this. You're still an interesting case, so it's really too bad. And now, my good friend, grit your teeth, it's going to hurt. It's going to hurt bad. He fired until Wohlbrecht didn't stir. Wimper looked to see that he was really dead, opening one eye with practised fingers. Too bad, he said. He probably would have made a good circus impresario in time. Wasn't he wild about midgets! It was almost pathological. Well, let's not speak ill of the dead.

Wohlbrecht is still lying there on the mountain-top, a one-legged skeleton. Without sacraments and unburied, alone and forgotten. The wooden leg, his faithful pet, still stands propped against the tree, exactly as it did then, waiting patiently for the resurrection of its master, which will surely happen some day. Any day.

Journey through the Night

What do you see when you look back? Not a thing. And when you look ahead? Even less. That's right. That's how it is.

It was three o'clock in the morning and raining. The train didn't stop anywhere. There were lights somewhere in the countryside, but you couldn't be sure if they were windows or stars.

The tracks were tracks – but why shouldn't there be tracks in the clouds?

Paris was somewhere at the end of the trip. Which Paris? The earthly Paris – with cafés, green buses, fountains, and grimy whitewashed walls? Or the heavenly Paris? Carpeted bathrooms with a view of the Bois de Boulogne?

The fellow-passenger looked still paler in the bluish light. His nose was straight, his lips thin, his teeth uncommonly small. He had slick hair like a seal. A moustache, that's what he needs. He could do a balancing act on his nose. Under his clothes he is wet. Why doesn't he show his tusks?

After 'that's how it is' he said nothing. That settled everything. Now he is smoking.

His skin is grey, that's obvious – it's taut, too. If he scratches himself it will tear. What else is there to look at? He has only one face and his suitcase. What has he got in the suitcase? Tools? Saw, hammer and chisel? Maybe a drill? What does he need a drill for? To bore holes in skulls? Some people drink beer that way. When empty, they can be painted. Will he paint my face? What colours? Water-colour

98

or oil? And what for? Children at Eastertime play with empty eggshells. His play with skulls.

Well, he said non-committally, putting out his cigarette. He crushed it against the aluminium, making a scratching sound. Well, how about it?

I don't know, I said. I can't make up my mind. Doesn't the fellow understand a joke?

Maybe you need a little more spunk, he said. Now's the time to make up your mind; in half an hour you'll be asleep anyway, then I'll do what I want with you.

I won't sleep tonight, I said. You've given me fair warning.

Warning won't do you any good, he said. Between three and four everybody falls into a dead sleep. You're educated, you should know that.

Yes, I know. But I got self-control.

Between three and four, said the man, rubbing the moustache that was yet to grow, all of us get locked away in our little cubicles, don't hear nothing, don't see nothing. We die, every last one of us. Dying restores us, after four we wake up and life goes on. Without that people couldn't stick it out so long.

I don't believe a word of it. You can't saw me up.

I can't eat you as you are, he said. Sawing's the only way. First the legs, then the arms, then the head. Everything in its proper order.

What do you do with the eyes?

Suck 'em.

Can the ears be digested or have they got bones in them?

No bones, but they're tough. Anyway, I don't eat everything, do you think I'm a pig?

A seal is what I thought.

That's more like it. So he admitted it. A seal, I knew it. How come he speaks German? Seals speak Danish and nobody can understand them.

How is it you don't speak Danish?

I was born in Sankt Pölten, he said. We didn't speak Danish in our family. He's being evasive. What would you expect? But maybe he is from Sankt Pölten; I've heard there are such people in the region.

And you live in France?

What's it to you? In half an hour you'll be gone. It's useful to know things when you've a future ahead of you, but in your situation . . .

Of course he's insane, but what can I do? He has locked the compartment (where did he get the keys?), Paris will never come. He's picked the right kind of weather. You can't see a thing and it's raining; of course he can kill me. When you're scared you've got to talk fast. Would you kindly describe it again. Kindly will flatter his vanity. Murderers are sick. Sick people are vain. The kindly is getting results.

Well, first comes the wooden mallet, he said, exactly like a schoolteacher . . . you always have to explain everything twice to stupid pupils; stupidity is a kind of fear, teachers give out cuffs or marks.

. . . then after the mallet comes the razor, you've got to let the blood out, most of it at least, even so you always mess up your chin on the liver; well, and then, as we were saying, comes the saw.

Do you take off the leg at the hip or the knee?

Usually at the hip, sometimes the knee. At the knee when I have time.

And the arms?

The arms? Never at the elbow, always at the shoulder.

Why?

Maybe it's just a habit, don't ask me. There isn't much meat on the forearm, in your case there's none at all, but when it's attached, it looks like something. How do you eat the leg of a roast chicken?

He was right.

If you want pointers about eating people, ask a cannibal.

Do you use spices?

Only salt. Human flesh is sweet, you know that yourself. Who likes sweet meat?

He opened the suitcase. No, I screamed, I'm not asleep yet.

Don't be afraid, you scarecat, I just wanted to show you I wasn't kidding. He fished about among the tools. There were only five implements in the suitcase, but they were lying around loose. It was a small suitcase, rather like a doctor's bag. But a doctor's instruments are strapped to the velvet lid. Here they were lying around loose. Hammer, saw, drill, chisel and pliers. Ordinary carpenter's tools. There was also a rag. Wrapped in the rag was the salt-cellar. A common glass salt-cellar such as you find on the tables in cheap restaurants. He's stolen it somewhere, I said to myself. He's a thief.

He held the salt-cellar under my nose. There was salt in it. He shook some out on my hand. Taste it, he said, first-class salt. He saw the rage in my face, I was speechless. He laughed. Those little teeth revolted me.

Yes, he said and laughed again, I bet you'd rather be salted alive than eaten dead.

He shut the suitcase and lit another cigarette. It was half past three. The train was flying over the rails, but there won't be any Paris at the end. Neither earthly nor heavenly. I was in a trap. Death comes to every man. Does it really matter how you die? You can get run over, you can get shot by accident, at a certain age your heart is likely to give out, or you can die of lung cancer, which is very common nowadays. One way or another you kick the bucket. Why not be eaten by a madman in the Nice–Paris express?

All is vanity, what else. You've got to die, only you don't want to. You don't have to live, but you want to. Only necessary things are important. Big fish eat little ones, the lark eats the worm and yet how sweetly he sings, cats eat mice and no one ever killed a cat for it – every animal eats every other just to stay alive, men eat men, what's unnatural about that? Is it more natural to eat pigs or calves? Does it hurt more when you can say 'it hurts'? Animals don't cry, human beings cry when a relative dies, but how can anybody cry over his own death? Am I so fond of myself? So it must be vanity. Nobody's heart breaks over his own death. That's the way it is.

A feeling of warmth and well-being came over me. Here is a madman, he wants to eat me. But at least he wants something. What do I want? Not to eat anybody. Is that so noble? What's left when you don't want to do what you certainly ought to do?

If you don't do that which disgusts you, what becomes of your disgust? It sticks in your throat. Nothing sticks in the throat of the man from Sankt Pölten. He swallows all.

A voice spoke very softly, it sounded almost affectionate: There, you see you're getting sleepy, that comes from thinking. What have you got to look forward to in Paris? Paris is only a city. Whom do you need anyway, and who needs you? You're going to Paris. Well, what of it? Sex and drinking won't make you any happier. And certainly working won't. Money won't do you a particle of good. What are you getting out of life? Just go to sleep. You won't wake up, I can promise you.

But I don't want to die, I whispered. Not yet. I want . . . to go for a walk in Paris.

Go for a walk in Paris? Big deal. It will only make you tired. There are enough people taking walks and looking at the shop windows. The restaurants are overcrowded. So are the whore-houses. Nobody needs you in Paris. Just do me a favour, go to sleep. The night won't go on for ever; I'll have to gobble everything down so fast you'll give me a belly-ache.

I've got to eat you. In the first place I'm hungry, and in the second place I like you. I told you right off that I liked you and you thought, the guy is a queer. But now you know. I'm a simple cannibal. It's not a profession, it's a need. Good Lord, man, try to understand: now you've got an aim in life. Your life has purpose, thanks to me. You think it was by accident you came into my compartment? There's no such thing as an accident. I watched you all along the platform in Nice. And then you came into my compartment. Why mine and not someone else's? Because I'm so good-looking? Don't make me laugh. Is a seal good-looking? You came in here because you knew there'd be something doing.

Very slowly he opened the little suitcase. He took out the mallet and closed the suitcase. He held the mallet in his hand.

Well, how about it? he said.

Just a minute, I said. Just a minute. And suddenly I stood up. God only knows how I did it, but I stood up on my two feet and stretched out my hand. The little wire snapped, the lead seal fell, the train hissed and screeched. Screams came from next door. Then the train stopped. The man from Sankt Pölten stowed the mallet quickly in his suitcase and took his coat; he was at the door in a flash. He opened the door and looked around: I pity you, he said. This bit of foolishness is going to cost you a ten-thousand-franc fine, you nitwit, now you'll have to take your walk in Paris.

People crowded into the compartment, a conductor and a policeman appeared. Two soldiers and a pregnant woman shook their fists at me.

Already the seal from Sankt Pölten was outside, right under my window. He shouted something. I opened the window: See, he shouted, you've made an ass of yourself for life. Look who wants to live. He spat and shrugged his shoulders. Carrying his suitcase in his right hand, he stepped cautiously down the embankment and vanished in the dark. Like a country doctor on his way to deliver a baby.

The Pious Brother

The Princess Ernestine von Trautenstein, having presented six sons to the Führer who had buried them one by one in Russia, was having her liberation ball. Balls were not infrequent at the Trautenstein Palace, which seemed to have been built specially for such occasions, and besides, the admission fee of five schillings helped defray the household budget. But this ball was almost like the good old days. Counts and countesses, princes and princesses had turned up in full force. It was a warm summer evening and excitement was in the air. The boarders, music students from Canada and England, were also invited. And of course Franz, the Jesuit and painter, who wore his cleverness on his face, plain for all to see. The Princess kept running to the gate. There was always something to attend to. Some thought they had been invited but hadn't, others had been but thought they had come to the wrong place. Not even the annual artists' carnival at the Künstlerhaus was as wild. By ten o'clock half the party was drunk, lying around in the freshly cut grass in twos and threes without a care in the world. Vodka was only three schillings fifty a bottle at the Russian store; admission was five, so there was no need to save on liquor. The sandwiches were being prepared in the basement kitchen by Prince Harald von Trautenstein in person. He kept his hat on and wiped the mayonnaise off his hands on to the loden coat he wore over his dinner jacket.

Around two o'clock the guests began to disappear. First

slowly, then faster and faster. And finally only those who lived in the palace were left, the Prince, the Princess, Ingelise and Albert, 'the children', and of course the boarders, John, Bernard, Lilian and David. Long before the noise died down, Franz was sitting in the kitchen having black coffee with Yvonne, a singer from London.

Franz was thirty-five, in the prime of life, a talented painter with his own studio in the heart of the city. That he belonged to a religious order was known only to the Trautenstein family – he had been giving Ingelise piano lessons for the last three years and had come to be regarded as a friend – and to Yvonne, who had heard it from Ingelise. Like all Jesuits Franz was a man of the world; he had lived a full life before embarking on the years of study that led to his ordination.

In honour of the occasion – the withdrawal of the Russian occupants – he had taken a drop too much. He needed the coffee to sober up. That was the price of abstinence. But it was almost a patriotic duty to drink to this liberation from the liberators. No one, not even a Jesuit, had the right to stand apart. It's not very often that the Russians move out.

Yvonne, who happened to be a Catholic from Scotland, had also drunk too much vodka. She knew nothing about politics and still less about vodka. She would have preferred a different kind of drink, like whisky, and another man, equally interesting, but neither was at hand; so she made do with what she had. Yvonne liked to seduce, everything else was too easy. She was well aware of this vice and admitted it freely. But never would she have confessed that her secret desire was to seduce pious Catholics and, most particularly, Church dignitaries. The thought of taking this handsome Jesuit's shirt off was almost as exciting as her early childish craving – she had been only eleven at the time – to crawl under the cassock of Father O'Connor, a cousin of her

mother's. Her room at home in Dunfermline was papered
with newspaper pictures of Church dignitaries.

Let other girls worship Clark Gable or Cary Grant; she
would rather have any parish priest or mendicant monk.
Priest or bishop, cardinal or Pope, the more prominent the
more exciting. The Holy Father, whose pictures occupied a
special place above her bed, was her favourite. To sleep with
the Pope and die – that was Yvonne's idea of God's paradise
on earth; the divine and the profane fused into one; 'in the
womb of love, at the bosom of happiness'. Yvonne was first
and foremost a mezzo-soprano. What did she know of sin,
what of religion?

It cost her such effort not to run her fingers through
Franz's hair that her right hand was beginning to ache. He
was so handsome, so slender, so tall, so virile. His fingers lay
long and sensual, slightly curved, with well-shaped nails, a
well-groomed hand, barely two inches from hers, close
enough to grasp. How she would have loved to squeeze those
fingers until he cried 'enough'. 'So gladly, oh so gladly.'
Where was that from? Schubert? Wolf? Mahler? – Bach,
why, of course. 'Oh, might I lie with thee, my sweet Saviour!'
Only Bach knew what love was all about, Bach was sensual,
he is the Don Giovanni of German Baroque.

Here beside her sat another. His name was Franz and he
was a Jesuit. But he was cool and impregnable (have the
times changed or the people?) and punctuated his long
commentary on the creation of the world with a sip of coffee.

The Creation and in particular the fall of Adam were
Franz's speciality, with which he drove women to absolute
submission, unconditional surrender: excited by his spiritu-
ality, driven to the brink of orgasm by his coolness, panting
with passion at his condescending, affectionate brotherli-
ness. In this way Franz, who had not touched a woman in
twelve years, obtained the simple satisfaction which he felt

was compatible with his vows.

Any dog or mole could achieve coitus. All it amounted to was a few grammes of liquid, and even that dried up in an instant. What did people know of the true opening, the opening of the soul, deep and dark as a well shaft? What did others know of the true fulfilment, the unusual thoughts, the corrosive analysis that one casts into the cistern like a plumb-line? – How deep is Thine abyss, O Lord? – How abysmal thy darkness, O world? – How loud is the echo of thy hidden fear, O man? – Yvonne was not Clara, the Jewess from Prague, who had slapped his face the year before. Yvonne was not Jewish. Only Jewish women have souls. Franz had no illusions about Yvonne.

'Out of His loneliness God created the world,' said Franz. 'He was lonely, because there was no one with whom to share the power of His glory. What is a God without men? Who is there to worship Him? Of course He could have held out alone until the Day of Judgment, for He is eternal. But without men, without the world, the universe would still have been chaos. The divine order, mastery of the tohu vabohu, the creation of man crowned His absolute power. So it was man who gave God His shape.

Except for the ascetic shape of Franz which affected Yvonne as an aphrodisiac, the topic itself left her absolutely cold.

He should have asked me first. Why didn't He ask me first?

What would you have advised Him? Franz asked.

The world is completely pointless, said Yvonne, at least for those who lack divine power.

Franz knew perfectly well what Yvonne would have done with divine power. She would have ripped his pants off. That, Franz knew, is how women are; either they expect violence or they want to use it. Women made him sick. What

108

did it say in his diary for July 17th, 1943? 'Slept with fourteen Ukrainian girls and women. Cost: fourteen slices of bread. Price of bread, thirty pfennigs – approximately two pfennigs per coitus. War is war.'

Franz observed Yvonne carefully. The way she pursed her lips appealed to him. Her white teeth were surprisingly good. When she wasn't speaking, she pushed out her lower lip and became a charming, pouting child. Her fingers were unattractive, too short, her skin was almost too white. The paint and powder were laid on too thick. Legs, thighs, and breasts probably just as white and transparent. Skin too delicate. Rabbit flesh. Physically she had nothing to offer, mentally even less. Too much naive good humour, too much childish playfulness, too sentimental, and too good-natured. Could she have a nose complex? Her nose is too thin, still, a complex is unlikely. Sentimentality comes from physical cowardice. That's something to work on. Inclined to hysteria. Good. Frighten, comfort, frighten. Might bring on a beautiful fit. Tears out hair, scratches, loses voice. Maybe a nervous twitch?

But she ought to be Jewish. Only Jewish women can work up a first-rate anxiety neurosis. His thoughts returned to Clara, the medical student from Prague. He liked the company of Jewish women. To the stupid ones he admitted only the Jesuit; to the bright ones, he also confessed the S.S. squad leader. Why not? They hadn't been able to pin any atrocities on him. And by the end of 1945 they had sent him home from the prisoner-of-war camp. Wasn't that proof enough? For seven years he had served the cause of Führer and Reich with fervour and unwavering devotion. But a thousand-year Reich that collapses in twelve years is devoid of every sound foundation. When the Führer committed suicide, he began to doubt. When Dönitz too capitulated to the Russians, his faith in the National Socialist revolution was irrevocably shattered. This scum call themselves the defenders of the West, bearers of the Germanic blood mission, but they shirk their sacred duty, to let the enemy, to his eternal infamy and disgrace, spill their blood, so that it might fall on him and his children, and his children's children. A Führer of the German people does not commit suicide – only a desperate unemployed house-painter from Vienna would do that. An oath sworn to such a creature is null and void, he deserves no sacrifices. Discharged by the Americans, Werner Bräutiger was doubly free, and immediately after his release, with the help of his S.S. company commander, Schacherl, professor of philosophy at Graz, he went into a monastery. He gave his vows to the Saviour Jesus Christ. For the sake of eternal life, he was only too glad to accept divine mercy and grace in exchange for the honour which went by the name of faith unto death.

Clara, where are you? Franz asked.

Yvonne's heart trembled with excitement. Here I am, she said. Right here. But my name is Yvonne.

Too bad, Franz sighed from the bottom of his heart. I raved to Clara about Alfred Rosenberg, just for the fun of it. Of course Rosenberg is passé. And she flew into a rage and slapped my face. How deliciously it hurt; it made me as happy as a child. What's the Knight's Cross compared to that? Jewess slaps S.S. man's face. This paradoxical, this almost uncannily impossible thing happened to me, to me. Death sentence to be carried out at once? – No, reprieve. Do I have some authority around here or not? Reprieve. I insist. Send her to Auschwitz for all I care. But give her time. Be humane. There's too much shooting going on in the Reich anyway.

The memory of this most grandiose of all times, when he held the life of others, especially women, in his hands, when he had rank and a gift for manipulating idiots, even if they happened to be his superior officers, this memory – was it really so long ago? – put Franz in a hypnotic state. He spoke as if in a dream:

Running the gauntlet, the bosom heaves, the whip cuts the flesh, but everyone is allowed through the black iron door, no one is denied entrance. The end of agony, the end of hunger, the end of fear. The room is crowded to bursting point, it all comes down to a question of space. An economy at war sets its own laws. Space, space, it's impossible to breathe. People suffocate almost as soon as they close the doors. So many bodies jammed against each other. Who are they, women shopping in a department store? No, stripped Jewesses in the elevator on the way to the last stop of German honour. Then Grace explodes, its name is Cyclone B. B as in Blessed. And ten minutes later – maybe fifteen, time hardly matters – life has gone out of their eyes. Nothing but naked dead female bodies, arms and legs intertwined. Dante's hell. Grotesque, obscene, cruel, magnificent like a Hieronymus Bosch. And Clara is among them – she's in the painting. The hand that slapped lives no more.

Yvonne didn't understand a word, her German wasn't up to it. It was barely enough for operas and lieder, plus whatever else she had picked up in the textbook *German for Foreigners*. Yet though she understood next to nothing of Franz's ravings, she was full of admiration for the wonderful sound of the German language. She was a musician first and foremost. And who on earth can understand these Germans and Austrians anyway? They never stop talking. They won't even let you eat without wishing you Gute Mahlzeit before and after, and they won't let you go away without saying Auf Wiedersehen or something of the sort a dozen times. She gazed at Franz and peered into his grey eyes, the most beautiful eyes she had ever seen: she studied his mouth that was made for kissing, and she didn't doubt for a moment that everything that went with it would turn out to be as it should. Will there be a chance soon? The way he looks at me. He wants to, sure he wants to. I could take him upstairs with me. But he won't dare. What if the Princess goes to the toilet, or Ingelise, it's too risky. Better wait. She could wait until he had talked himself to shreds – what's left belongs to me.

Franz looked deep into Yvonne's eyes until she couldn't help blinking, and thought of the Jewess from Prague who, instead of dying in Auschwitz, had given him the most glorious slaps of his life. At each slap he had whispered inwardly: 'She forgives, she forgives.' Chastised with love, oh vanished dream of childhood. Alive or dead, Franz thought, God didn't provide us Christians with a soul. All we know is how to kill, not how to suffer. We haven't the soul for suffering, even our Saviour had to be taken from the Jews. One of us wouldn't have worn the crown of thorns. He hated and despised – and prayers were no help – the insensibility of his Christian world, just as once upon a time, long long ago, he had hated the Jews for their weakness.

In a Europe with scarcely any Jews, his hatred of the few pitiful survivors had seeped away. There was nothing left, nothing but the fervour of prayer and the paling images fashioned by a great era out of flesh and bones – images such as no Bosch could ever create in oil and water.

Gone, gone forever. The moans have died away. I am a man alone with God. Yvonne. Yes, of course, Yvonne. One scream of her lust until my ear drums burst . . . Are you going to scream, Yvonne? – Very well, I'll talk.

And Franz talked of Adam and the rib. God created Eve from Adam's rib and not the other way round as the psychoanalysts claim. They are always looking for hypotheses. Adam rape his mother? It's out of the question. Years later incest was punished with death. If Eve had been Adam's mother, God would have had to destroy Adam on the spot as an example. But He did nothing of the sort. Ranke was wrong, so was Freud. The first Church Fathers lied even more shamelessly, though actually they say pretty much the same thing as the modern psychologists. You don't forfeit paradise for the sake of sexual intercourse. Adam's sex life wasn't sinful in itself, what was sinful was Adam's independence, his sexual maturity. After tasting the apple Adam saw that the fruit of the tree was the fruit of Eve's womb. Eve was pregnant. This meant that Adam could create life just like God. And this was what the Father couldn't put up with. He drove him out of His house because He saw that His creature had grown up and become His equal. Not as punishment, but because He realized that His work was indeed finished. God showed Adam the door in order to make him learn to bear his own responsibility. Why did the theologians suppress this aspect of free responsibility and put all the emphasis on the curse of earthly existence? For a very simple reason. The Tree of Life – Adam, by the way, had no time to eat of it – would have bestowed immortality on him as well. That would have been going too far. Man would have lost his desire to beget children and it would have been all up with the divine magic. To have to die is inevitable but cruel, and one fears it. It's like being unborn, Adam tells himself. In the dark, foul-smelling womb of the earth. It is pointless to live with such death as a prospect. So the theologians persuaded man that there is a paradise, hence no need to fear death. But, man asks, what is this paradise like? *Like before the Fall.* So by way of explaining paradise, what it was and what it might be, the theologians call existence a curse and a vale of tears. But that's not what God intended when he banished Adam. It's a cruel invention of Jewish and Christian scholars who lacked the imagination to understand the divine purpose. The result was a Christian world of torpor. Any pagan, any Buddhist is a thousand times superior to us. The Jews at least rescued human responsibility and the Buddhists saved God's omnipresence. All that was left to us Christians was the mystery of the Trinity; take that away and we are finished.

The long speech had nearly sobered them both. Yvonne hadn't understood a word. He is religious and I am sinful, he is serious and I am silly. How marvellously frivolous this Jesuit makes me feel, how divinely irresponsible. And she sighed with such passionate desire that Franz felt it in the marrow of his bones.

Silent and unnoticed, the Princess had listened to Franz's last words from the doorway. – Don't let me interrupt you, children, she said, and sat down at the table. She poured herself some coffee. But as Franz had come to the end of his speech there was nothing to interrupt. Edifying, very edifying. The Princess loved to be edified. Whenever she heard the word God, regardless of the context, a pious shudder came over her.

The death within three years of six sons ranging from twenty-one to thirty-five had driven her back to the bosom of the Church. Getting Constant, the last one, to go had been difficult. The others hadn't dared to open their mouths when she commanded them to volunteer for the S.S. ('The Führer needs you, my sons.') But Constant had played sick for weeks. First it was tonsillitis, then earache. And then stomach trouble. A strapping, vigorous young fellow, a little pale from too much night-life, but otherwise in the best of health. Hysterical fear she called it. She had had to lift him out of bed with her own hands like a baby. 'Aren't you ashamed of yourself? You call yourself a man?' The same afternoon she had delivered him with his belongings at the recruiting station.

She saw him once more, in the uniform of an S.S. Panzer Grenadier, raising his arm in the Hitler salute as he and his men were passing before the party leaders in a victory parade after the fall of France. He did not see her. But she was proud of him, of his sunburned face, his hardened manly features, the steely glint in his blue eyes. Here was a man, not the child she had known. A soldier of the Führer. How well he looked in uniform, better than in a dinner jacket.

It was the last time. Although he was stationed nearby until the Russian campaign, he never showed up at home. She was without news of him until the twenty-fourth of June when the telegram came. He had fallen the very first day – the will of Providence. He was the first of the six. The news had shaken her only when, three years after the war, his battalion commander had told her the truth about his death. By his own carelessness he had slipped while boarding his tank and had been crushed under the treads. Only the immediate family knew, and they kept the secret. Constant just didn't have the makings of a hero. He had taken after her father who in the First World War – an Austrian general! – had surrendered to a gang of Serbian bandits, who had made short shrift of him, strung him up on the nearest tree.

Constant was the first. The other five followed, one by one. Not one received the Iron Cross. She never got rid of her mourning clothes. Johann, the eldest, was last to die, while fighting partisans. Such was the will of Providence. There is no arguing with God.

Franz loathed the old woman. She was a spider. A venomous spider. Ingelise had told him about the six brothers. If I'd had a mother like that I'd have killed her. That woman is insane. No amount of prayer could lessen his hatred of the aged princess. And there was no one with whom he could talk about it. The mere sight of her paralysed him with disgust. The spider princess.

Princess von Trautenstein was not exactly attractive. She was very tall, about six feet. Her face was bluish-white and bloated. Her eyes were two slits pressed downward, their colour impossible to tell. Her nose was long and fleshy, rather like a tapeworm, her lips were full, and her teeth first-rate dental work. Only the wrinkles under her chin betrayed her seventy years. Dressed up, she seemed no more than fifty. Her best feature was her grey hair. Her hands and feet were enormous. Her feet were encased in gigantic low-heeled shoes. She was wearing something black – she always wore something black – made of velvet and simple cotton. It was neither dress nor skirt and blouse. Her bare shoulders were covered by a simple fox fur. Princess von Trautenstein had trouble with the letter 's'. After using it she forgot to remove her tongue from between her teeth. It stuck there.

Franz made a point of addressing the Princess as Excellency, concealing his revulsion beneath an excess of politeness – he always derived a secret satisfaction from the irony of it. – I beg your pardon, Excellency, said Franz jumping up – I do beg your pardon. I should have left long ago.

The Princess smiled graciously. – Why, Franz, you mustn't, it's so seldom that I have a chance to chat with you. The stupidity of everyday life. The duties of the household. Who can afford servants nowadays? – No, please do stay a while. One never has time for quiet reflection. Maybe it will be different now that the Russians are going. Except for their cheap food, they brought us nothing to be thankful for.

If your Excellency is really not too tired, said Franz. The old bag had ruined his evening. All he had got out of Yvonne was a sigh. What of the sighs to come? And the orgasm? Spiders induce coitus interruptus. Even the old Mayan myths tell of that. The spider goddess von Trautenstein squirts poison into the cohabiting prince, and in the very act his member curls up, withers, and dies.

The Prince has gone to bed, the Princess lisped. Albert and Ingelise have gone to the Rasupovskys for coffee.

116

Tomorrow is Sunday. The children don't go to Mass anyway. No, please stay, Franz, the house is deserted and I love to listen to you. You are the cleverest man I've ever met.

Please, please, Franz protested, embarrassed. He couldn't stomach compliments from an arch-enemy.

Don't you think so, Yvonne? She smiled at Yvonne. Though she was the uncontested darling of the family – the only one of the boarders allowed to practise in the ballroom – Yvonne wished the old witch, as the students called her, ten feet underground. She would have liked to say something affectionate to Franz; she might even have used the same words. But now everything was ruined. There wasn't much left of the night. And this Franz needed time, time and patience. She understood his glances. No one was as fascinating as this man. What worldliness! And to think that he is a member of the Church. She began to shiver and tingle.

Or is his worldliness as deceptive as his dress? He wasn't even wearing an ecclesiastic's collar, he had a tie on. Still, his shoes, suit and socks were black. Clothing proved nothing. To be a Jesuit proved nothing. Yvonne knew from experience that what mattered most in love was opportunity. Time and patience. There was an oppressive silence, lasting no more than a few seconds.

You are an artist, said the Princess to Franz. She licked the coffee from her lower lip, lest it slide down her steep chin into her décolleté. Will you please explain one thing to me; I should so much like to know why our Saviour is always represented as a soft, gentle, I might almost say effeminate man. A man who could chase the moneychangers out of the temple with a whip, who had the physical strength to carry His own cross up a mountain, cannot possibly have looked like that. I refuse to think of Him as a weakling. I've wanted to ask you that for ages.

Three o'clock in the morning and the old monster wants to

know everything. How he hated her. She had ruined his plans. Franz sought Yvonne's eyes and to his consternation detected a roguish gleam of complicity against the Princess. Had he given himself away? That damned liquor. No self-control. He must have nothing in common with Yvonne, not even contempt or hatred. Any sort of complicity would wreck his plans. This little English girl must be made to writhe with passion, to throw herself at his feet in confusion and despair. But he could do this only if he remained absolutely cold, sternly aloof. How would he be able to say no and brush her off like dust if he entered into a conspiracy with her?

The evening was wasted. All he could do now was to give her his address before leaving. The Princess's presence didn't disturb him. It was generally known that Franz led a blameless life, though no one knew why. The word had spread around town, for he received ladies in his studio at all hours. They dropped in with conscious designs like Yvonne (because only difficult conquests are worth bothering with), or with an open mind (because my studio is a natural place for women to spend their time in), undecided whether to seduce this clever, good-looking man or to be seduced by him. They came at all hours of the day and night, and spread word of his chastity. So there was no harm in giving Yvonne his address while the Princess looked on. The thought cheered him up. And it gave him time to think up an answer to this most hackneyed of all questions. *Jedem das seine*, to each his own, Franz remembered, and a diabolical desire overcame him. The spider must be crushed. This was his chance. Maybe his last.

Excellency, Franz began softly, you are perfectly right, of course. The effeminate Saviour is a falsification. A product of the Renaissance. The old Greek frescoes represent Him as the powerful, robust type He must have been. The Saviour

118

was well built and muscular. His features were hard and taut, the look in His eyes was noble, almost masterful. He was a virile man. In every respect.

The Princess was pleased. She gave a slight nod. That was just how she had pictured Him.

Franz continued. It was the Renaissance that first painted suffering into Jesus' face. For suffering in the human countenance was just being rediscovered as was man himself – eighteen hundred years after the destruction of Greek civilization. Industry, then in its infancy, needed human beings, not slaves. Artists needed the human face, they needed what is most human and most appealing in man, namely suffering. And where did they find the living models all painters – except the abstractionists – need? They found the expression they were looking for in the innocent victims of the Inquisition, in the unsuspecting, tortured eyes of the Jews. And they gave that expression to the Saviour, whose suffering until then had meant nothing to them. The face of the Redeemer, himself a Jew, was copied from the victims who for His sake were being burned at the stake in Spain. That is the greatness, the ironic truth of art. Sometimes they made his hair blond, sometimes black, usually they straightened his nose, but what they were really interested in was the expression. That expression, that pain, the pain of innocence, burned in the eyes of the Jews. And in theirs alone. Now do you understand how that sickly, tortured look came into the healthy face of the Saviour?

The Princess did not understand a single word, but she loved everything connected with religion. Though she would rather not have had the Jews brought into it. For after all they had started the war with their intrigues and forced Hitler to defend himself. So that they were really to blame for the death of her six sons.

Go on, the Princess commanded. It's very interesting. Her

idiotic politeness was getting on his nerves. I'll have to put it more plainly, draw a picture, so to speak.

Excellency, said Franz. I have seen a photograph of your son Constant. Princess Ingelise was kind enough to let me see it; she gave it to me, in fact. It was taken two weeks before the Prince entered the Army, in November 1939. He was just twenty at the time. I have used the picture as a model for a painting. The painting is finished. It's the best I've ever done. A friend of mine has photographed it for me, because it's going off to an art show. I have a reduced copy here in my wallet.

Very interesting. Fatigue made her speech-defect positively painful. – May I see what you've done with the old photograph? Most interesting. Franz took a photograph from his wallet and put it down in front of the Princess.

When the Princess laughed, it sounded like an unsuccessful attempt to ring a rusty bell. A kind of croaking. The Princess laughed until the tears came into her eyes, she always cried when she laughed. Franz affected to take offence. – I assure you that allowing for a minimum of artistic licence, my painting was done faithfully after the model. – The Princess had put down the photograph but she was still laughing and kept repeating the words 'rogue' and 'prankster'.

Yvonne arose. She just had to see what had brought on this hysterical laughter. But she could see no reason. All she could make out was a young man with a beard, a bald head, earlocks and a skull-cap. This son certainly bore no resemblance to the Princess, he had big black eyes. They looked more like the Prince, though she had never really noticed his. Or had she never looked? That must be it. After all, a son has to look like somebody.

The image of his father, said Yvonne, meaning to be jovial. This was too much for the Princess. There were limits to everything. She stood up. She seemed to be eight feet tall, to touch the ceiling.

Take your miserable Jew boy and leave my house at once. I repeat: at once! – you too, Yvonne.

At once! the Princess screamed. Don't talk back. I won't have it. My son, the Prince, died at the Russian front, he was an officer in an S.S. Panzer regiment. You, a former comrade in arms, ought to be ashamed to desecrate the memory of the dead.

Franz saw there was no point in trying to say anything. There was foam at the old woman's mouth. She'll die of a heart attack. No, he didn't want that to happen. He couldn't have that on his conscience. The joke had gone too far. She is an old woman. I've got to tell her the truth even if it sticks in my throat. Nothing is lower than cowardice. He turned round in the doorway and said:

Excellency, I confess. That picture is not your son, it's not even a copy, I realize . . . I beg your forgiveness. I will tell you the truth: It's a young Jew named Eliezer Gross whom I shot with my own hand in the ghetto of Lodz. *This is the only human being I have on my conscience.* He had refused to turn his sister over to me. That is the truth. I've had the picture with me ever since. It reminds me of certain things and I thought it might cure you of your grief, I thought we might forget our sorrow together.

Get out! screamed the Princess. Leave my house, you, you degenerate!

Franz bundled Yvonne out ahead of him. In silence he pulled her after him half-way through the city. They climbed the four flights of steps to his studio in the dark. He didn't want to be seen. Not tonight. The studio was under the roof. It had two enormous windows offering a view of nothing but the sky. As a painter and a Jesuit, he had no need to see anything else. Never had Yvonne seen such a studio.

Tausky, the stage-manager, would have to come and look. What a setting for Mimi. Not even the cast-iron stove was missing.

I'll make you some coffee, said Franz and vanished behind a curtain. Fully metamorphosed into Mimi, Yvonne went from picture to picture, humming to herself. She cast a glance at the bed. It was wide. I wouldn't want to die of consumption in it, she said to herself, everything else is all right. As to the pictures – some were as big as the window – she couldn't make head or tail of them. Smears of harsh colours. Nowhere a man or even a tree. Modern. Maybe he'd like to have models but he is not allowed to. Maybe that's why he makes all these smears. Too abstract. Abstraction is all right but this is too much. What about that coffee? – Not a sound from behind the curtain. Nothing. She began to feel afraid. She could have managed very nicely up here for a few weeks. But he is a bit of an eccentric. Eccentrics are interesting. She tiptoed to the curtain. Maybe he's saying his evening prayers, praying God to forgive him for the sin he's going to commit with me tonight? She opened the curtain and screamed. She screamed until her breath gave out. Franz lay on the floor, blood gushing from his mouth. His eyes were wide open and staring. He was wrapped in a yellow-and-black silk shawl, fringed at the border, embroidered in gold round the collar. He had on a little false beard and a wig that made him look bald, with long hair at the temples.

The Princess was not surprised when she received the news of Franz's suicide. – He hadn't been right in the head lately, she said. But secretly she took to lighting seven candles instead of six at early Mass, and included Franz in her prayers. For after all, he too had served the Führer in the S.S. A comrade in arms of her sons was like another son to her.

The Judgment

It can't go on like this. And he was right. Because the execution had been set for the seventeenth of June and here it was the eleventh. In his position there wasn't much you could do with six days. Since the highest authorities had rejected his petition for pardon – that had been three days ago – he knew what he was in for. Dying didn't worry him, now he was scheming revenge. At his special request neither his parents nor his fiancée were admitted to the prison; they stood outside the main gate, carrying a shopping bag with food they had brought. And they gave interviews to the press. He couldn't care less. Everybody, he told himself, must die. There's no mercy. He'd never had any either. He'd killed twelve, all women. They had screamed like stuck pigs, not one enjoyed it. But dying is dying. That's life.

The last one, Gertrude was her name, had scratched his face, the bitch, but he'd showed her. Just out of spite, he had let her catch her breath three times; it was fun watching her. Now she thinks I'm going to let her live – hell, no! – and he had squeezed again. He did it three times. Serves her right. You don't scratch your murderer's face. Scratching hurts, the scab is there for five days. He'd done in twelve of them. Twelve in one year. A murder a month. Not a bad record. They had discharged him on December 31st (manslaughter, clobbered the bastard kid for yelling so loud while drinking his milk), and on the first of January he went to work. The first of every month. First of February Hilde – first of March

Frieda, and so on. On the first of December he was finished. Since the first of December he hadn't killed a soul. His hands itched when he thought of it. In six days it will all be over. Where was he to find the thirteenth? Thirteen is a lucky number. Got to make it thirteen.

Mass-murderer Schnabel's thirteenth victim – that's what the headlines will scream. Murder at the foot of the gallows. The Lichtenfeld strangler at work again. He could still teach these guys from the papers a thing or two. What did the *Abendblatt* call it last time? Midnight murder. Those jerks from the paper think twelve fits in with midnight. Christ, are they stupid.

Just to get away from those crummy headlines, Schnabel would have been glad to drop dead on the spot. But it's not so easy to drop dead. Especially six days before you swing.

Revenge. Revenge, Schnabel whispered. Revenge is sweet. Revenge, revenge. The sound of the word made his mouth water. The word felt delicious on his palate. There ought to be more words like that. Then maybe things would have turned out different.

Today was the eleventh. It was nine in the morning. He had made his bed, put his cell in order. He wasn't hungry. He was allowed to smoke. He threw himself on the bed. Ordinarily I'd have gone swimming, said Schnabel to himself. It's hot today. You can see by the look of the air. Suddenly he saw the water. It was blue-green. The trees were all part of the horizon. He lay in a rowboat (two schillings an hour) and breathed the water. White clouds up above. The water lapped against the wood. It was peaceful. Wonderfully peaceful. The bicycle bells and barking dogs along the shore didn't break the stillness. Not at all. Things can only be so warm and peaceful when the background noises are right.

His boat drifted down the quiet Danube. Air, water – a

heaviness came over him. He fell asleep.

In his dream he saw himself sleeping. And because he was asleep, failed to notice that the clouds were coming closer and turning greyer. Grey, greyer, light-black, black. A drop fell, he caught it on his tongue, then a second – his tongue was still out but he couldn't count any more – the drops came pouring down the hill, all of them at once. A cloudburst, a deluge. The thunder nearly split his eardrums, then he could hear nothing, the rain fell like dull blows. Lightning flashed wildly through the air. Wind lashed the boat. He rowed with all his strength but made no headway. No land in sight. He had to bale with one hand. I won't drown, he kept saying to himself. I won't drown. Not me. And then he lay in the water. The wind had tipped the boat. He swam as hard as he could. He swam for his life. I'll get a gold medal. I'll beat them all. Nobody can keep up with me. When it comes to swimming, I'm okay. But when he reached land, the land was gone. Another flood. Dikes is what they need, not these damn kitchen gardens. The land was gone all right; here and there he ran into a rusty weathercock. Damn gardens. Disgusting. What they need is dikes. Land.

He swam, literally ripping the water out from under him. And still there was no land. Trees, but no land. And only the tips of the trees.

I'll eat those tree-tops like new spinach. Land is what I need. Ground under my feet. Tree-tops belong in poems. I've got power. I'm strong. Nobody can swim like me. Nobody. Suddenly he was cold with fear, but he was so wet he didn't notice that he was sweating. Nobody. With one hand he reached down to his swimming trunks. Well, thank God. Thank God. That's what drowsing will do to you. Can't trust this summer weather. First it's hot and then you drown. Maybe it's only the water that's got my swimming trunks so blown up? That can happen. He reached down

125

with both hands. And even after long searching he couldn't find a thing. Then he drowned – glug-glug – help, help – and woke up.

Damn it, Schnabel grunted and jumped up. Only a few days to live, and I get smutty dreams. Disgusts me. Suddenly he was seized by a strange thirst, as if his mouth had been rubbed with hot sand. First I'm too wet, then I'm too dry, he thought, for he saw no difference between waking and sleeping. Maybe it's because I've only six days left. How do I know? Might as well get it over with. The wait was getting on his nerves. And all the fuss they were making because he was only twenty-one. As if age had anything to do with it. You're much better off hanging while you're young. If I were old I'd feel sorry for myself, Schnabel told himself. Later on memories weigh you down. They fasten on to you like leeches. Leeches. He liked the word. A young man hangs easy. It won't hurt. And suppose it did, going to the dentist isn't any fun either. Don't be a sissy. Where does it get you? No sissy would have chalked up twelve (the kid's death had really been a mistake). He had only hit him to make him shut up. If that's all it took to make him croak, it only goes to show he wasn't much good. Sickly children never get anywhere in the world anyway. Schnabel had never been soft, he had never pampered himself. At the age of five he had chopped off the little finger of his left hand on a dare. They didn't believe he would do it – that's why. He'd wrapped the finger up and hidden it for weeks. Six months later when his father had started beating him again, the sympathy had worn off, he had picked his nose with the dead finger half wrapped in a handkerchief. His father's eyes had popped. His mother's too. Give me that finger, his father had yelled. This minute. Give me that finger, you no-good bastard. He had put up a heroic fight. It's my finger, he had screamed, see, it fits me, and he had held the shrunken stub in its old place. His father turned scarlet and damn near had a stroke. Give me that finger this minute or I'll call the police. If a father can't take a finger away from a kid without the police, his authority is shot. You can kiss my ass, he yelled at him, and he calmly began to scratch his ear with the dead finger. His father flew into a blind rage and knocked him cold with an uppercut. When he came to, the finger was gone. He had never forgiven his father for that. On the very first day of school he had left the schoolhouse by the back door and disappeared for good – until his grandmother died – he was ten years old and she died while chopping spinach, he found her lying beside the kitchen table, and then he'd had to go home again. Revenge, revenge, Schnabel screamed when he thought of his father – it's him; it's all his fault. He's got to be the thirteenth.

The idea gave him such joy that it hurt. But how do I get him here in this rat-hole?

Schnabel was a man of action. When he had an idea, he acted on it. He wasn't one to put off things. Never had been.

He pounded on the iron door with his fist. Two guards appeared. They always carried loaded pistols. Schnabel was known in prison as the most dangerous character they had ever had.

Bring me pen and ink, he ordered. I've decided to make my will. Schnabel had special privileges, especially since some women's club – the president was a first cousin to the Minister of Justice – had got the whole country stirred up over the 'sick murderer of Lichtenfeld'. In all the cities signatures and pennies were being collected for him.

He sat down at the table, feeling like a top executive composing a personal New Year's greeting for each member of his staff. To be run off in three thousand copies.

Dear Warden, he wrote. Their guns at the ready, the guards watched every stroke of his pen through the peep-hole.

I, the undersigned Karl Schnabel, Prisoner No. 3454345 at the local prison, beg and request you respectfully to please kindly grant and/or approve a last request. As your Excellency probably knows, I was sentenced to death by hanging due to twelve murders. The sentence, as I have had the honour to have been notified, is ordered to be executed on June 17th of this year, on my person, by which means I will expiate with my life for my deeds.

As perhaps your Excellency knows and has been informed, I have neither repented nor confessed. But now that the day, so vital for me, is looming nearer, and in every probability I will not have no opportunity to confess and/or repent afterwards, I hereby beg to request you respectfully to consent to permit me to speak in privacy for a maximum of fifteen minutes with the man to who I am indebted for my life, my own personal father, Franz Schnabel. As I desire to give a last account of myself, but only to my father – in the hope of being allowed and privileged to face my heavenly Father with a clear conscience.

I promise to pay back your Excellency in the other world as soon as possible, presumptively no later than twelve o'clock, being that I expect to get up there by approximately nine Thursday morning. I take the liberty of respectfully wishing to point out that a maximum of fifteen minutes in privacy with my father will suffice to soften my stony unrepenting heart.

Please kindly inform me, at this address, as soon as possible, because the time will soon be expired.

Respectfully,
Karl Schnabel, Mass Murderer

He was pleased with the letter. He put it in an envelope, sealed the flap carefully to keep those lugs from reading his letter, addressed it: To His Excellency the Warden of this Prison, and gave it to the guards.

Then he pissed resoundingly against the wall, because now he could do whatever he liked.

The warden read the letter and gave it to the chaplain. He in turn passed the letter on to the assistant warden, and he to the captain of the prison police. The four of them sat in the office, smoking. This was a matter they could not decide by themselves, Schnabel was too important. Under the circumstances – every day outside the prison, the cousin of the Minister of Justice made a speech that was promptly published in the papers, side by side with editorials such as 'Why Schnabel must not be pardoned' – the four thought it advisable to consult the prison doctor. Dr Maurer came in, read the letter, shook his head – at the grammar – and said: Why not? The warden gave instructions. To avoid attention the father would be brought in disguised as an inmate. Brilliant. No one would ever suppose the visitor to be old man Schnabel. The press would not be informed until two days later.

The warden rang. A guard appeared. Bring me a prison uniform with cap. The prison uniform with cap was produced. Who's going to take it to old man Schnabel? The deputy warden volunteered. He'd have his picture in the papers. His friends would take a more respectful tone.

When? asked the police captain. When should I open the gate? Ten o'clock at night. Tomorrow, said the warden. Safety first. At ten o'clock there's nobody outside. By that time people have their bellyful of murderers.

But suddenly the chaplain had an idea; all his ideas came to him at the last moment. But suppose, he asked, the father doesn't want to see his son? No one had thought of that.

After much noisy confusion, they reached unanimous agreement. The chaplain should go along. For spiritual support. And without delay. The two climbed into an official car. When they got to the crowd, they stopped. This was the Schnabel residence. The crowd pressed round the car. There was nothing to see but plenty to talk about. The bundle with the prisoner's clothes was thought to contain the dead man's effects. The chaplain had come to comfort the family.

The bloodthirsty villains, they've probably strung him up already. The government always lies. This proves it once again. A young reporter wrote busily (he had no paper handy) on his cuffs.

Five minutes later the two men came down again. Still carrying the bundle. The wife must have refused it. To torment a poor woman so. If the police hadn't intervened, the crowd would have beaten the two men up. Quickly they vanished in their official car. With the bundle. Because the father was not at home. He was holding a press conference, his third, at the Café Altinger.

At the Altinger the two had to wait. To escape notice, they withdrew to the furthermost corner. There was nothing about them to arouse suspicion. The chaplain was in civilian clothes except for his white collar, and the assistant warden had on an ordinary black suit. They ordered black coffee and tried to catch something of the conference that was being held in the back room. They waited patiently, it was their duty, but there was nothing to hear.

Old man Schnabel left the press conference like a diplomat, shaking hands to right and left, hands of sympathy, hands moved by the sincere respect which is the due of every celebrity.

The assistant warden and the chaplain pulled him into their corner. The father had to be on his guard against autograph hunters. What can I do for you? he asked condescendingly. They explained. That wouldn't be so easy to decide. Himself, yes, sure, but he'd have to ask his wife and future daughter-in-law. Could he have until next morning to think it over?

A decision of such importance had to be slept upon. As for the prison clothes, nothing doing, they could stick them up . . .

Old man Schnabel paced back and forth, so as to understand himself better as he pondered. Mrs Schnabel was silent. The daughter-in-law leafed absently through a fashion magazine.

I know what you're thinking, Fanny, said Schnabel to his daughter-in-law, and what you're thinking too, he said to his wife. As for myself, I don't know what to think. If I see him, I'll have to control myself, if I don't see him, I'll reproach myself for it. And you'll reproach me even more. You'll leave me no peace as long as I live. So I'll see him. And then I'll clout him one. Bringing such disgrace on his parents. We know whose fault it is that he turned out like this. I'm not going to argue – you spoiled him, Mitzi, you always gave in to him. It's all right, I don't want to argue.

But the boy's going to hang and after all he's my own son. It's too late to clout him, though that's what he deserves. Keep quiet, Mitzi, I don't want to argue. You can see I know what's what, but that's how it is, we've raised a criminal. Even as a child he was crazy. I don't want to argue. But he deserves to be killed. I know what you want to say, and what you want to say, Fanny, I know too, you're getting me all mixed up, now I don't know what I want to say myself. Yes, he deserves to be killed. But not by the government. It's his father that ought to kill him. Don't get excited, that's the truth. I brought him into the world, and I'm the only one that has the right to take his life. I've got to kill him. What business is it of the government's? The child belongs to me.

He's my son – some son. A mass murderer isn't a son. We gave him plenty of love, we've nothing to feel guilty about. Maybe we gave him too much, but I don't want to argue. The government thinks he belongs to them, just because they've got the gallows. I don't need any gallows. I'm going to strangle him. An eye for an eye.

That's the only sensible thing to do. A father has to take the consequences, or he's no father. Let the government punish our children? Where would that get us? It's none of the government's business. What do I care about the penal code. He has sinned against his seed. And that's me.

At this thought the father went wild. He had never seen so plainly what it means to be a seed. It made him hot and cold all over. The responsibility almost crushed him. I was your seed, the father screamed, and you let me down.

Don't be a pig, I won't stand for that dirty talk. Fanny closed the fashion magazine and stood up. He killed my kid, so now the law's going to kill him – won't be nothing left of you people and that's all right too. With these words she buttoned her jacket and disappeared. Mrs Schnabel sighed.

At ten o'clock he was informed in writing: 'Petition granted.' Karl Schnabel was in high spirits, he had had an excellent night. Hardly dreamed at all. Today was Sunday. The weather was fine again, his petition had been approved. What more can a man ask for? Everything was going as he wanted and it won't be long till Thursday. He was almost looking forward to it.

Four thirty: Wake up, wash, dress. Mustn't forget to shave, good rubdown with cologne. Smells nice. Four forty-five: breakfast. He had ordered a nice breakfast for himself – Prague ham and grapes, real class. Then clean-up; got to be neat. Blankets good and straight, chair against the wall where it belongs, then another piss, because it's the last time and later there won't be a chance. And at a quarter to six they'd come and get him.

He steps out of his cell in his best suit, despite the early hour some gentlemen are standing there in black, they're not coming for the funeral, so what's the black for? The coffin is ready, the lid lying beside it. As long as it isn't too short, won't look so good with my feet pulled in. And then up the two-three steps. He'll be smiling, that's for sure. Let them know he don't give a damn. Everybody looking solemn except him. Everybody's got a guilty conscience except him. Can't see the hangman's face, has his hood on, like in the history books. They blindfold him, why the secrecy? He didn't blindfold his women, the best part of it was the look in their eyes as they died. But a private citizen isn't the same as the government. The government's ashamed to look a man in the eyes.

Then the rope goes on. It tickles but you don't die of that. And then you swing, that's what does it. Two hours later, Schnabel told himself, I'll be up there. Where, he didn't know. And why it takes two hours and not six, that was something else he didn't know. It'll be about half past eight, he said to himself. What's a few minutes one way or the other?

Karl Schnabel was in the best of spirits – because tonight he was getting his thirteenth and thirteen is luck, a Jew had told him that in a café in Mariahilf. Jews are known to be smart. He wouldn't do business with them but they're smart all right.

The day couldn't pass fast enough for him.

The thirteenth will give the papers something to write about. Never happened before in a death cell. Fame, celebrity. Schnabel had discovered immortality.

Then came the knock.

Karl jumped up. The door was opened. Two ruffians with drawn revolvers led his father in. The peep-hole was left open.

Close it, roared young Schnabel. So they closed it.

He can't help him escape, they said to themselves. They've searched him, he hasn't any poison or string. They've even taken his comb away.

They stood face to face. Father and son. Mass murderer and his seed. For two minutes they said nothing.

Well, said the father.

Well, said young Schnabel.

You wanted to talk to me, said the father.

I got nothing to talk to you about.

But I have, said old Schnabel.

You won't talk long, young Schnabel roared, and had him by the throat.

He squeezed. The old man squeezed too. Strangling's what you need, the old man hissed.

What about you, said the son.

And they throttled each other.

The elder Schnabel had stronger hands. He squeezed until his son's eyes popped out of his head.

When the guards came in, the younger Schnabel was dead.

You won't have to hang him now, said the elder Schnabel as they put the handcuffs on him. Do what you like with me. The one that gives the seed has the right to punish – nobody else.

An anarchist.

Old man Schnabel was not sent to prison but to the lunatic asylum, and even there they didn't keep him long. The judges were understanding. They all had sons, and besides, the government had saved itself twelve hundred schillings.

The Window

When her behind left him cold he knew it was all up with love. Brasil took the blankets into the living-room, he would have taken them even if she had woken up, and lay down behind the television set. The wind shook the panes. The floor wasn't exactly soft and the carpet tickled. Bladder pressure set in when he thought about her behind. He crossed his legs, that helped. He felt nauseous thinking about her behind, and conjured up others, big ones, white ones, soft ones, broad ones, open ones and closed ones. The more he thought of them the sicker he felt. I've got to talk to somebody, he thought. Something's happened; they used to put him to sleep, now they kept him awake. Something's happened. Can't go on like this. Every night behind the television set, for all he knew there might be spiders crawling across the floor.

Brasil made a dash for the door. When the pressure on his bladder had gone he turned on the light. He looked with pleasure at the flowers and the colourful spines of the books, the colour scheme was right, it all showed good taste. Everything was just right, the curtains too. So were the paintings, he had nothing to reproach himself with in that department. It was all familiar, a cosy, comfortable home. Everybody has his backdrop. And he looked round. There they huddled, thirty millions, children and old men, all thrown together in the enormous apartment house, each behind a window, a slit in every curtain, standing on each other's backs like the musicians of Bremen and peering into the darkness. Thirty million windows, there may be even more, but he couldn't crowd any more people into the building, not if he tried, and sixty million eyes piled up pair over pair. No wonder he couldn't sleep. Then he thought about her behind again and about love. Every love. Every single love. When he couldn't stand it any more he crept to the curtain, opened it cautiously, and pressed his nose to the pane. There was the man – by calculation he was due for his red-striped pyjamas today – wearing his red stripes on schedule and looking out. Now was his chance to talk. Like a fish in a bowl, he said: Do you look at my window when I'm not looking out? And the other, likewise turned fish, said: It's the first time in ten years and the second time since I've been living here.

We really must get together. Let's meet at the corner. And the other said: I know a café, it's noisy, but we can talk there.

I've got to speak to you about behinds, won't that bore you?

Nothing bores me, said the man in the red stripes, except maybe sleeping. Let's meet. I like to talk about earthy things. I'm religious.

He withdrew from the window and stepped into his trousers. He pulled a shirt over his head and slipped into his heavy coat. He found his shoes in the box marked 'Cleaned'. After putting his slippers in the box marked: 'Not cleaned', he went out into the street. He had forgotten his socks.

The squat shadow of the man in red stripes was waiting on the corner. They shook hands in silence. Red stripes also wore a heavy coat. But he had on socks and even a tie.

That was fast, Brasil whispered.

Yes, said the other. I'm always fast, I never undress.

And the pyjamas? asked Brasil.

I wear them over my suit, the other admitted. My wife

136

insists. Even if you don't sleep, she says, a man's got to wear pyjamas. Why argue? Why not do her a favour? Now we fight about different things. Marriage is a compromise. Hence the pyjamas. Everybody has to pay. I don't have to work. My wife came into a bit of money. That's why I said 'yes', I had to gain time, now I've got plenty. I had to find God. Now I can't sleep at night. Because I've found Him. He leaves me no peace. All night I think of God.

Red stripes took him by the arm and pulled him round the corner. The street was poorly lighted. At the end of the street he said: We'll take a cab.

Brasil felt bad about the whole thing. How was he to get a word in? Better try right now, he decided. If I wait, my turn will never come, the night will be over, and I won't have had my turn. Behinds, he said in a loud voice. Her behind leaves me cold. What do you say to that?

The importance of the statement wasn't lost on the other. Her behind leaves you cold? That's amazing. And you're still a young man. At my age everything will leave you cold. I used to believe in breasts. Now I believe only in Him. He is holy. He understands. He likes caresses. Everybody knows that.

Mr Brasil didn't want to be talked to. He wanted to talk. It used to be difficult, now it's easy, maybe that's the trouble. I don't know. But suddenly it was finished. Without love I don't want it. The carpet tickles. It's hard, even if it is a soft carpet. Not hard for a carpet, hard for a bed. What's the use, I tell myself. It's no good without love. I'm not an idealist, I don't believe in God either, God doesn't keep me up nights.

Where are you taking me? They had come to the main street. The taxi was waiting.

Take us to the Mill, said Mr Leander. The driver knew the Mill and started right off.

I don't know the Mill. Your usual place?

Yours too, said Leander. You're in for a surprise.

They said nothing more. The Mill was open, but not very lively. They went up three steps and down a narrow corridor. On the walls newspaper clippings of girls. You could hear the music as soon as you reached the corridor. The Mill was a nice place, the tables were clean, the lamps on them had cheerful shades. A radio was playing. The bar was at the far end. Behind it stood a stout woman with bleached hair, throwing dice. She smiled as they came in.

In a corner sat three customers talking in a loud voice. Shit, said one, a cadaverous man with slicked-down hair. Yes or no, shouted the second. He looked like a professional soccer player. Not tonight, yelled the third. They were drinking some colourless liquid out of little glasses which they refilled from a bottle under the table.

Shit, I say. Yes or no. Not tonight.

The voices grew louder, the glasses emptied faster. Shit. Yes or no. Not tonight – went the refrain. The two sat down near the entrance. They hadn't come to spend the night, just to talk.

Quiet, cried the woman. You ought to be ashamed. The voices grew muffled. Shit. Yes or no. Not tonight, they whispered.

Mr Leander threw back his head, indicating the men. Every night it's like this. They can't agree.

What do they want? asked Brasil.

Anarchists, Leander whispered. They want to blow something up. At my request. Probably a church. How do I know? Anyway I've notified the police. They're being watched. But as long as they can't come to an agreement, nothing happens. Anarchists, bad lot. Useful at times.

It was all the same to Brasil. Church or parliament. For his money, they could blow up the whole city. He had something more important on his mind.

What do I do now? He liked Leander, he trusted him. There's something respectable about a man who can't sleep on account of God, even if he's not as important as he makes out.

What'll we drink? asked Leander.

Cognac, said Brasil.

Two liqueurs, called Leander. The fat woman stopped laughing and went for the bottles.

Cognac, said Brasil.

Liqueur is better. Leander rejected all arguments. The liqueur tasted like peppermint but went straight to the entrails and a second swallow to the tips of the toes.

Good, isn't it? After the third sip Brasil saw nothing but Leander's burning eyes under ponderous eyebrows; they pierced his heart.

It's good all right, was all Brasil could say.

Leander took half a cigarette from a case and began to smoke. He didn't offer the case. Brasil didn't smoke.

Before you begin, said Leander, and probably meant just what he said, I want to tell you right away: I'm religious, whatever you have to say, don't forget that. I won't stand for any nonsense about God. I just want to make that clear. To avoid misunderstanding. After all I don't know you. You live across from me. But what do I know about you? Don't say anything bad about God or I'll beat hell out of you.

Apart from that, we can talk about everything. You can even talk about God, but nothing nasty. I'm serious. He took another sip.

I'm serious too, said Brasil. Her behind leaves me cold. What am I going to do now? We married for love. Twelve years I've been married and not for the inheritance. Out of pure love. She had a behind, well, I didn't want another. And I wasn't a virgin. She was right, that's all. Do you understand? I had lived before. Then I ran into Georgette.

And Georgette knew what matters in life. Love. Just the two of us. Love for love. I could have married other women, for money, career, anything. But I was smart, I married for love. And now it's finished. I'm not smart any more, as of tonight. How do you think I feel? I could cry if I could, though we're childless but happily married.

Crying is no good, said Leander. Love is up here. He pointed to his forehead. You've got to have God. Without God it's no good. I've already told you I used to believe in breasts, a man needs breasts, I thought. If he hasn't any of his own, he needs a woman's. Nothing came of it. What are breasts compared with God? You've got to hold on to breasts and then you fall asleep. But God, my friend, holds you and doesn't let you sleep. That's something. God can do everything – He made a man of me. God has everything, breasts have nothing. God is love, breasts are mostly milk-glands. Same with her behind. It's only flesh. It leads to nothing.

Can you hide in it, for instance? Of course not. You always know where you are, because you can't see yourself. But when you hide in God, it's different, you don't know where you are, because you're everywhere. It's like broad daylight. You're there, but you don't see yourself. A hole is just that and no more. Who can put up with that? But God is love, cried Leander, pounding the table with his fist.

Why should I hide? Brasil didn't understand. From whom? Who's looking for me? Who needs me so badly?

That's just it, cried Leander so loudly that the three men turned round. You hide and you don't know why. Because you're blind or want to be. You're afraid. Afraid, that's what it is. And all of a sudden you're not afraid any more and you feel awful. That's no miracle. But that's the very thing a man in your situation needs. Still, it's never too late.

For me everything is too late, Brasil moaned. If love is gone, no God can help.

For Brasil had always been an atheist. He didn't believe in any God, much less in the Son of God. If Christ in person had stepped into the Mill and sat down beside him, he'd have taken him for 'some funny-looking foreigner'.

With me it's love or nothing. Now I've got nothing. He took a sip. The stuff was delicious, a heaviness rose from his toes to his knees. From just one sip. Before his eyes he saw a white cow and three Chinamen with long pigtails. It's all symbolic, said Brasil, especially the Chinamen.

They're anarchists, said Leander. Watch your step with them. The police have been notified. Just the same, Brasil, I like you, even if you are a heretic. I'll make you a proposition.

Brasil took another sip. It was like a light going on inside him. The white cow, he said, is she holy? Two more! he called to the bar lady. She came waddling up with the bottle and smiled.

Leander drained his glass quickly so as not to be late for the second round. I'll make you a proposition, Brasil, we'll switch places.

Brasil was far away in the stars. These Chinamen, Leander, you don't mind if I drop the Mister – he didn't wait for an answer – these Chinamen, Leander, maybe they're holy too. Who knows?

We'll switch, said Leander. About the anarchists, you're right. They are.

And the cow?

You're right about the cow. She is.

Holy? asked Brasil.

Holy. My word of honour. – About this switch. I'll take your place, whispered Leander like a spy. I'll take your place.

Impossible. Though drunk, Brasil knew what the other was getting at. I can't do it. She'll notice.

Leander clutched his arm. Friend, he said gravely, may I say friend?

Please do, said Brasil. He liked him more and more. The Mill is my place from now on. To hell with her behind.

Friend Brasil, have you a first name?

Arthur. The Chinamen are getting up. What's that they're carrying?

The three had indeed stood up from their table and were coming closer, step by step.

Arthur, I'll tell you the honest truth. The Chinamen are bringing me something. The three were standing across the table.

The soccer player said: Sweetheart – take this. He handed Leander a hundred-mark note.

The cadaverous one with the slick hair who looked like a partridge gave Leander a gold cigarette case. Take this, beloved, he said.

Leander's manner was one of indifference. And you have nothing? he asked the third.

The third was a squat man in his fifties. He had a bulbous nose and two tusks. This is all, my Saviour, he said, holding out a change purse. Not much in it. Had a bad day.

Brasil thought he was dreaming.

You know them, he cried in terror.

That's nothing new. I've known them for a year. They worship me.

Worship you? Anarchists?

Why, yes, said Leander with indifference, the truth must be told. I am He.

You are He?

A new incarnation. Yes, my dear Brasil, that surprises you. You think I'm a neighbour, just somebody across the way, somebody you see in the window; actually I'm the Redeemer.

Heavens above, Brasil went pale. You're right. You are He.

Leander turned to his worshippers. I have a job for you.

At your service, your Grace, said the soccer player with a bow.

Bring me a female without a behind. For my friend.

Honoured, whispered the partridge.

As you command, my Prince, said the one with the tusks.

Leander waved them away.

Being God, my friend, I can help you. Lucky for you. Man, are you lucky to be living across from me.

Brasil rubbed his hands for joy.

Leander, my dear friend, I didn't believe it and I still can't take it in. A woman without a behind, that's just what I need. Will I see her?

In ten minutes, Brasil. You've been waiting twelve years. What's ten minutes more?

A woman without, Leander. That would be a miracle. But I guess it's nothing for a God.

He poured down the rest of the liqueur. Leander also drank up. Two more, he called. The bar lady, smiling, came over with the bottle. Like it, gentlemen? She filled the glasses.

White cow, said Brasil, I like your Mill. In a little while I'm going to see something – something nobody ever saw.

Leander will give you anything. But watch your step. He's not always so nice. And when he is, he wants something in return.

He can have anything from me. Drunk on happiness and liqueur, Brasil beat his breast. What do you wish, my Saviour?

Wait a while, said Leander. If I deliver my promise, you'll give me a little something. Meanwhile let's drink. It shortens the wait.

Brasil drank one and then one more. He didn't collapse. He didn't get sick, but he could have sworn that it wasn't a bar they were sitting in but heaven. He floated on air.

Hey, I can fly, said Brasil.

Everybody here can do that, said Leander disparagingly. Don't bother to. Your miracle will be here any minute.

I can fly, cried Brasil, climbing on the table. He took one step and jumped. The next moment he was hanging from the lamp.

Careful, cried the bar lady, if it falls, you'll have to pay for it.

Brasil, who would never have dared to imagine, let alone attempt, such a thing, grew bumptious.

I can fly, he cried gleefully. The next moment he was sitting over the door. It can't be, it can't be, he cried.

Come down, cried Leander, don't be so bumptious. Save your strength for later. You won't believe your eyes.

Brasil glided through the room and landed feet first on his chair. It's weird, he said.

Here she comes, cried Leander. Voices were heard in the corridor.

Now about the little something? You promise to hand it over? We don't want any arguments later.

Whatever you wish, my Saviour, my Redeemer.

And one more stipulation. The woman stays here. You can't take her with you.

Whatever you say. I feel happy.

The three entered, preceded by a blonde creature of seventeen. She stepped up to Leander and Brasil.

I'm Trude, she said. What can I do for you?

Then we've got it straight, Leander interrupted his new apostle's gaping. If I keep my promise, you'll give me the little something.

I feel happy, cried Brasil, to hell with the rest.

144

Undress, Leander commanded. The girl began to undress.

Brasil felt queasy. She had neither breasts nor nipples, not even a navel, and no sex. Turn round. Leander ordered. She turned round – Brasil's teeth chattered. From neck to thigh there was nothing but smooth sunburned skin, no hips, no curvature, no dividing line.

His tongue hung out with amazement. It's not possible, not possible, he said. May I touch her?

All you like, said Leander. I never welsh. Brasil ran his hand over the skin, it felt normal, perhaps a trifle oily, but perfectly normal. A smooth flat board covered with skin.

Marvellous, he cried, marvellous, I want her.

You can't have her, said Leander, you can only look at her.

The girl turned round several times, like a model presenting new fashions. She was pretty and had a charming smile. But the body was absolutely unreal.

How on earth can she walk? Brasil wondered.

Don't you worry, my good friend. You saw her come in. She didn't fly. She walks all right. Are you satisfied now? Get dressed, he ordered. Trude dressed. Thank you, said Leander. Come and pick up your money on Friday.

Brasil stared at Leander in amazement. He had seen God, he could fly, he had seen a woman who couldn't exist on this earth – his nerves were shot. His whole body trembled as if in a fever.

I guess you're kind of exhausted, came Leander's voice benevolently from afar. Now, my friend, I get my price. You know what.

I can't, said Brasil. I can't do it.

You're not going to keep your word? Leander looked at him sternly. A man without honour. Have I kept my word?

Yes, Brasil stammered. But to tell you the truth, I couldn't imagine it.

Your imagination seems to be as deficient as your honour. And you're not only stingy, you're selfish. Give it here, roared Leander. He took a penknife from his pocket and laid it on the table. Out with it, he shouted. Quick.

Brasil was terrified. His knees wobbled. They were alone in the bar. The three and the girl had gone, the bar lady seemed to have vanished into the back room.

All right, said Brasil. I'm ready. Take it. I've been a fool.

Leander shut the penknife and put it away. Your willingness, my friend, is enough for me. That's all I need. But next time it will cost you more than a little something.

Don't get mixed up with me. Don't go to the window to see if I'm there. Because I'm always there. That's the truth. I never sleep. Never.

Now go home to your wife. And whether it makes you sick or not, don't tell anybody. It's me at the window. Nobody else. Remember that.

Brasil thanked his friend, deeply moved by his generosity.

But if you need me again, my friend, just come to the Mill. They always know where I am.

Brasil took a run and, winged with new passion, flew over the night roofs of the city the shortest way home. He has been a new man ever since.

Hurrah for Freedom

Don't get your hopes up and don't expect too much – the man who said these words was named Leonard Balthasar and weighed close to twenty-two stone. Everything about him was pale and fat – even his moustache. Without the moustache he might have been taken for a fat old woman.

You'll meet my women if we hurry. Yes, I say women, two of them are my sisters, one is my mother. We live out here, all seven of us.

How come seven? asked the other Leonard. For he too was named Leonard – they had made the discovery, to their mutual delight, after they had gone less than fifteen miles. The second Leonard was deeply grateful to the fat one. But for him he'd never have got out of Lund. Now he was looking forward to a warm bed, coffee and cigars, and breakfast. It was bad enough in the daytime, at night nobody stopped to pick you up.

How come seven? – Because we've got three children. Used to be seven. We slaughtered four. Swedish sense of humour, said the second Leonard to himself. But he was a medical student from Vienna and nothing could fluster him. So he asked: Nothing else doing at your place?

Oh sure, said the fat man. There's plenty more. We're nudists, we've got a pig in the cellar, and a dead horse hanging from the rafters.

That was a little better.

Balthasar, said the second Leonard, is that Swedish?

No, Lithuanian, said Balthasar. When the Germans cleared out, so did we. My father couldn't make it. Or my uncle either. Forty-four of our relatives were deported to Siberia, two were shot. That's the Russians for you.

We've been living here for fifteen years, it's a good country, nobody meddles in other people's business. Quiet, civilized people. Discreet. Yes, this is what I call a country. You can stay with us as long as you feel like it, but there aren't any rooms. We've torn down the walls, the stairs too. More space that way. Beds, yes, we've got those. Are you tired?

I guess I am, said the second Leonard.

And you're studying . . . ?

Medicine. In Vienna. Ah, medicine – in Vienna. I know Vienna. I was there for six months, during the war. Beautiful city, fine opera. I'm crazy about music. Do you travel much? You students are always travelling around. If you get to Russia some time let me know, I can help you and there's something you could do for me.

I'll be in Russia in two weeks, said Leonard, going by way of Stockholm, Helsinki and Leningrad. But from Helsinki I'm taking the train.

Really, said the fat man, really, then you're a gift from heaven.

The house stood all by itself in a forest, though not a dense one, and there was a village within a mile and a half. It wasn't as out of the way as he had imagined.

By the time the two crawled out of the car – help me, young man, cried Balthasar – it was twelve o'clock. It was drizzling but not cold. There was light in the house.

Mother! called Balthasar. The door opened and a fat woman stood in the entrance, holding a pair of slippers. Otherwise she had nothing on.

The house was really large, or rather high, there were no
148

doors or windows, no stairs either, as Balthasar had said, it was very spacious. Let's undress, said Balthasar. It's too warm in here. And indeed the stone flags were almost steaming. It wasn't just warm, it was hot. Balthasar took off one piece of clothing after another, in the end he had nothing on but the slippers the naked old woman set down at his feet. From the far corner of the room the place was enormous and only sparingly lighted, two feeble bulbs hung down on a wire from far above, voices were heard, first one, then another: Are you there? cried a woman's voice, is it you, Leonard? cried another.

Yes, it's me, cried Balthasar, and I've brought another Leonard with me. A medical student from Vienna, he's going to spend the night here.

Two female figures detached themselves from the wall, both naked, both fat. One might have been forty, with a squint in her right eye, the second was about thirty and had black hair. They looked him up and down. Leonard felt ashamed when he noticed he was still dressed. He put down his knapsack and began to undress, keeping on only his watch. The women smiled. Here was a well-mannered guest, no need to explain the customs of the house. The one with black hair went to a cupboard and came back with slippers. They'll fit you, she said. The floor is too hot without them. Leonard put on the slippers, they were warm and lined. He looked around. There were two tables and a few chairs, several couches, and all sorts of cupboards, all the furniture was lined up along the walls, that was what made the place so spacious. There was a television set and even a piano. There were flowers in each of the eight windows.

The place smelt of flowers, hyacinth and jasmine, but it also smelt of something else.

Leonard looked up towards the ceiling and there it was hanging from the beams. A horse. The bones were beginning to protrude from the flanks. The three women and Leonard followed his glance. Three years more, said the woman who had opened the door, she was maybe sixty and her breasts hung down slack to her navel (she was the mother).

Three years more and we'll have the skeleton.

A Lithuanian custom? Leonard inquired.

Only with the Balthasars, said Balthasar. But let's sit down.

The children are asleep, said the one with the squint, we mustn't talk too loud.

They all took seats at a round table to the right of the windows. Beside it there was an ultra-modern sink, aluminium and teakwood, a refrigerator, and a washing machine. Pots and pans hung on the walls. They were in the kitchen. The mother went to the cupboard and came back with a large stone jug. We make our own kvas, she said, and poured him a cupful. Then she poured some for her children. The daughters drank only to be polite, just so they could get a good look at the guest.

You've come from Vienna today? asked the one with the squint. From Lund, said Balthasar. He's a medical student. His name is Leonard too. I couldn't let him sleep on the highway. It's too dangerous nowadays, said the one with black hair, the papers are full of it. There's quite a lot of crime in Sweden, you wouldn't have thought so, would you? Only last week, said the mother, a man on a bicycle was attacked near Ödeshög, first robbed, then stabbed. Sweden's not what it was before the war. We used to come here often, the children were little then, but who'd have supposed we were going to end up here? — The Russians deported my husband, he died in Siberia, did Leonard tell you? Yes, said Balthasar. He poured down the kvas, he was hot and thirsty. After the first gulp the second Leonard couldn't go on. He could have sworn the stuff tasted like blood diluted with lemon juice.

Ach, the Russians, whined the old woman. Deported forty-four relatives, shot two. My husband's dead, I know that. Why don't you drink? – we make it ourselves. It's fresh.

Is there blood in it? Leonard was curious to know, if only for his diary.

Stuck him today, said the elder sister. Once a week we draw off four quarts. You wouldn't believe how he thrives on it. Tell him, Vera.

That surprises you, said the younger. Hog's blood mixed with the kvas, that's what makes it a real drink. My brother introduced it here. He learned it from a Finn during the war.

He was a shepherd, said Balthasar, shepherds have the old folk-wisdom, they've got tradition too. I was way up north for the reindeer market. There wasn't any market, no more reindeer either, the Wehrmacht had used them up long ago. The shepherd, his name was Eino, was lying in a hut, just about smothered in his own shit, the lice were running across the floor like ants. He was nearly starved to death, all he had was a drink – he called it kvas – it was pure blood, human blood, the day before he had stuck a knife into his two children, couldn't stand to see them starve. Wartime, see, the Wehrmacht didn't have anything either, so Eino had to live on his children's blood. Before the war, he told me, they'd always drunk hog's blood, the taste didn't bother him, but it got him down to be drinking his own children. He didn't last long anyway, little kids haven't got much blood. I gave him a loaf of bread. When I came back two weeks later – I had to go way up to the coast – the bread was untouched and Eino was dead.

So now we drink hog's blood to his health. It's cheap and very nutritious. Skoal – Balthasar poured down another cupful.

Mother, bring us something to eat. The old woman got up

and went to the refrigerator.

Now I understand about the hog, said Leonard.

As a medical student he mustn't let anything upset him, it was a matter of professional dignity, he owed it to himself, but the horse . . . Why the horse?

I'll explain, said the old woman. She set down a bowl of pickled meat. Have a bite to eat. She gave him a big chunk, it was covered with onions and swimming in oil and vinegar. It's almost like home, Leonard thought. He took one bite, then let it be. He could have sworn it was human flesh. But Balthasar had tied on his napkin and was eating with gusto, shovelling in such big chunks he could hardly close his mouth. The dressing ran down over his chin.

The horse is in memory of the old country. My husband was a horse-trader. We had to leave everything behind, the farm, the animals, everything. We couldn't sell a thing – the Russians got there too fast. The first thing they did was to requisition the horses. They gave us a receipt. The old woman had tears in her eyes. We left next day, you can't fool with the Russians. We were sitting in the wagon, looking back. Tina, the mare, was lying not ten paces from the yard, with her tongue hanging out, shot. She'd run away from the Russians, she wanted to follow us. They didn't have time to catch her so they shot her. That's the Russians for you. Yes. That's the liberators.

Four years ago we bought the horse and hung it up there in memory of Tina, in memory of the old country. And when it's all rotted away and only the skeleton is left – Lithuania will be a free country again, the Russians will be gone to hell.

Yes, now we're just waiting for the skeleton, it can't be long now, said Balthasar between two bites.

We're refugees, said the squint-eyed one, looking up at the horse with her good eye. Refugees have got to be patient. Am I right?

And the stink? asked the second Leonard.

The flowers take it away, said the younger sister, and you get used to it in time. Our people have to put up with worse under the Russian boot, it stinks to heaven of corruption and slavery – a dead horse in the house is the least we can do for our country.

The old woman just sat there with tears in her eyes. Balthasar had stopped eating and belched a few times to show he'd enjoyed it.

That was Hedda, he said. – No, Hedda was finished long ago, said the elder sister, that was Martha. You don't even know your own flesh. – This must have been a good joke, for they all laughed. We'll keep Arno for Sunday, mother will cook him up into Carelian soup. – He won't be as good as my Werner, said the younger. – You and your Werner, fumed the elder sister. You and your Werner, my Arno was prettier. – Prettier, hare-lip and all, laughed the younger. – You hold your tongue, cried the squint-eyed sister. Nobody's going to say mean things about my boy. – Quiet, cried the old woman. Say something, Leonard.

Leonard Balthasar banged the table with his fist. What's our guest going to think of us, behave yourselves, girls. Who'd you get the kids from? Well, out with it.

From you, Leonard, stammered the elder. – Yes, of course, from you, said the black-haired one.

That's more like it, said Leonard Balthasar, picking his teeth. You see, the children are all from me.

Leonard the Second felt slightly sick in his stomach, he had taken a bite. Human flesh, children's flesh – he was going to throw up. No, he said to himself and took a deep breath, a medical man can't do that. A philosopher – yes. A medical man has to control himself. But I've got to get out of here and quick. He stood up, the others stood up too.

You're not leaving? said Balthasar. Where can you go

tonight? It's warm here.

Too warm, said Leonard. He wanted to be polite, but he couldn't manage it. I've got to be going. You're cannibals.

Cannibals. He reached for his clothes and dressed, he couldn't do it very quickly. Balthasar held him by the arm. A cold shiver ran through his bones.

You mustn't leave like this, Balthasar said gently and menacingly. The old woman came between them. Listen please, Mr Student, we might as well tell him. Tell him, tell him, cried the sisters. We're poor refugees, said the old woman. All these things you see here, washing machine and all, were given us by rich relatives in America, they gave us the car too. – She was crying again. – They gave us everything. Except something to eat. My daughters had no trousseau, my son didn't have a nickel. How could they get married? But people want children. We haven't anything to eat, just the vegetables and potatoes we grow out at the back.

People want a piece of meat. That's what happens to poor refugees (now the two daughters were crying too), reduced to eating their own children.

That's what it comes to.

Then why don't you go home to Lithuania? Leonard was losing control.

To Lithuania, to the Russians? Do you know what you're saying? – They dragged off forty-four relatives to Siberia, shot two. My husband's dead. We'll go back to Lithuania after the next war when the horse is a skeleton. You don't know the Russians, that's easy to see. – Yes, the squint-eyed sister joined in, that's easy to see.

The noise woke the children, they jumped out of bed and pressed against the women's legs. The children were from three to five years old, each of the women picked one up to comfort it. Out of sleepy eyes they looked distrustfully at the clothed stranger. The youngest, a blonde girl of three, began to cry. Stop that, said Balthasar. The child fell silent at once. In this house they don't threaten the children with punishment, thought Leonard. They have to do as they are told.

The seven naked creatures stood around him, in his clothes it was stiflingly hot, they all had bloated white bodies (and all the women were without pubic hair, another Lithuanian custom?). Leonard felt as if he were dreaming.

He was rather sorry for them, a well-dressed hunter on safari can't help feeling sorry for the savages he meets. He would have liked to give them a handful of glass beads or a mirror. They are poor and proud, Leonard said to himself. Actually, what did he himself know of the Communist yoke – all hearsay. Here for the first time he was seeing the real victims. They moved him almost to tears. But a medical man has to control himself.

True, they were naked, they ate their children, and the whole house stank. But in the paradise of workers and peasants, as his newspaper said, the people were still worse off. And besides, they're not allowed to travel.

In two weeks I'll be in Russia, said Leonard. He wanted to make up with Balthasar, after all he had given him a lift. It wasn't their fault if their diet disagreed with him.

Yes, said Balthasar, I wanted to talk to you about that. But I see you're in a hurry. Just do me one favour, ask for the first Lithuanian, there are still a few of our people in Russia. And the first Lithuanian you meet, here's what I want you to say to him: The Balthasars are fine. They want for nothing. The Balthasars wish you confidence in the future, in a few years there'll be war, the skeleton will be finished, and Lithuania will be free again.

Please remember all that when you get to Russia and meet any of our enslaved brothers or sisters.

Leonard promised. To escape from hell he promised everything.

155

The naked Balthasars waved after him, long after he had vanished in the woods, on his way to the highway, on his way to Russia. He was tired, but glad to be all in one piece.

That's what insanity is like, thought Leonard, as he fell asleep by the roadside, but none of my friends will believe a word of it. All medical men.

Resurrection

'Deum Jesum Christum in gloriam eternam est. Nu.'
Goldschmied turned over on the other side, put down the
prayer book and tried to sleep. He pulled his coat over his
head and nearly suffocated, he took it off and the light hurt
his eyes. He turned from side to side, but cautiously, so as not
to touch either of the walls. His head touched the wall behind
him (it was padded) and his toes pressed against the chair
between the bed and the fourth wall. He couldn't sleep a
wink. They won't let you have your rest, not even in the
coffin, you'd expect there'd at least be room to stretch your
legs six foot underground. Not a chance. Psiakrew Pieronie!
It was only in Polish that he dared. As a Protestant he wasn't
allowed to swear. I hope he's a midget, I'll put him under the
bed. How can two people sleep in this place? A hundred
guilders a week and he won't let me breathe. Meine goyim.
Czort!

Swiss Alpine Club. Holiday at Arosa. Altitude 6,000 feet.
First-class hotels. Reduced prices out of season. It's out of
season all right. Who wants to go to Switzerland in October?
Too early for skiing, too late for sun-bathing. Now would be
the time to go, if I could. The calendar won't mind. He
himself had brought the calendar. Every day a stroke. So far
he had struck off 184 days, 184 years. Only the pencil had
stayed untouched by it all. It hung on its nail, its point as
sharp as on the first day.

The motto for October: In golden splendour flows the

wine – and the picture: vinter carrying a basket full of grapes, clinking glasses with a young couple. Carriage, vines, women, a team of oxen in the background. Young woman smiles merrily. Husband smacks lips. Vintner holds one hand over his paunch.

I could stand it in Switzerland right now. Not too hot, not too cold.

In November they plough, in December they sing Holy Night, Silent Night beside the Saviour's cradle, in January skiing, in February too, in March they take the cable car up the Matterhorn (does it have to be March?), in April the young lambs playing in the meadow, in May a nightingale singing in the trees, in June they ski and swim.

But how will I live through such troubles?

Nothing about it in the calendar. A book tumbled down from over the bed. *Introduction to Inorganic Chemistry*, Dr K. Kluisenhart, Groningen 1902. In 1902 I was still in Cracow. Do I need inorganic chemistry? I'm inorganic enough already. He put the book down and took paper and pen to write van Tuinhout a letter. Dear Mr van Tuinhout: Nothing doing. I can barely stand it by myself, if there are two of us I'll go mad. I'll give you a hundred guilders, but don't do that to me. Find him another place.

I'm a sociable man, but how can two live in this hole without killing each other? Besides, there's the difference in denomination. Try to understand.

He didn't write the letter, he didn't have time. Van Tuinhout was outside the wall. He gave the prearranged knock. Without having to get up, Goldschmied opened the two hooks.

The trap door was pushed up slightly from outside and van Tuinhout climbed through the opening. Now what does he want? Has he found two more?

As usual van Tuinhout sat down on the bed without a

word and for a time said nothing. Van Tuinhout was a pale man, about forty-two, thin hair, short straight nose and small brown eyes. When he spoke, he usually stuck his tongue out as though to give his words a last lick before he let them go; when he was silent, he played with his false teeth.

Meneer Goldschmied, he said finally: not tomorrow, tonight he'll be here. Right after dark.

Thank God, said Goldschmied, I would have had a sleepless night. Van Tuinhout eyed Goldschmied with suspicion. He had taken in roomers for fifteen years, but a Protestant, religious too, by the name of Efraim Goldschmied, origin unknown except that he was a *mof*, a German – that was a new one.

Whatever Goldschmied said in his mixture of Yiddish and Dutch sounded suspicious to van Tuinhout.

How old is he? asked Goldschmied.

Not more than thirty. Maybe twenty.

You mean there's no difference? Nu, we'll see. But remember, you promised. A week at the most, it'll get to be three – then I'll kill myself.

Meneer Goldschmied, it isn't my fault. I have to do what they tell me. It's only a week, 'then they'll put him somewhere else.

Did you protest at least, van Tuinhout?

Of course. But that's how it is. We can't be finicky. It's getting more dangerous every day. And the Jews have got to be helped.

You're telling me? Of course they've got to be helped, but does that mean putting two grown men in a box? Why, this isn't a room, van Tuinhout, it's a coffin.

It's not a coffin, Mr Goldschmied, you're always dramatizing, it's a closet. Where one can live, so can two – don't get me wrong – but that's how Mr Jaap and Mr Tinus want it. You think I have anything to say about it?

Suppose something terrible happens, Mr van Tuinhout.
You'll be responsible.

Responsible? In the first place the Germans are responsible, in the second place Mr Jaap and Mr Tinus. I'm just
carrying out orders.

Silence set in. What can I do with this goy? He's an idiot.
Goldschmied rubbed his three-day beard. (Every three days
he was allowed to use the bathroom in the rear hallway.) It
can only end in disaster. That much he knew. A hundred and
eighty-four days he had lived through it – and what's to
prevent the war from going on for another twenty years?
Cholera! He'd never live to see the end. A young fellow in the
same hole? Two corpses in one coffin would have more room;
besides, corpses wouldn't mind. Van Tuinhout didn't
budge. He sat there with his hands in his pocket (it's not that
cramped in here), stared straight ahead and seemed frozen.
He didn't smoke, he didn't seem to be looking at anything,
he just sat there. After four minutes Goldschmied began to
feel uncomfortable. He knew exactly what was going on, but
now that he had something to complain about, he didn't
want to play along. He too waited four minutes, he too put
his hands in his pockets and stared at the wall. I can outlast
him at this any time. Goldschmied said his twelve Our
Fathers. That's more than he can do. How can that man
think nothing so long? He gave himself another dozen Our
Fathers. Still van Tuinhout didn't budge.

Till the Last Judgment I'll let him sit, Goldschmied
decided. He'll get his money anyway, but this time he can
beg for it. Van Tuinhout gave a slight cough. Ah, he's
starting in. Goldschmied gave a little cough too. (In this hole
'coughing' meant an almost inaudible clearing of the throat,
and 'talking' meant a barely intelligible whispering.)

So make up your mind. Spit it out.

Van Tuinhout would rather have hanged himself than

remind Goldschmied of his rent. Goldschmied knew the ritual by heart.

It was up to him to start in about the homework. Then came lamentations about Kees, the poor motherless boy, followed by a short speech about the moral degradation of children in wartime, and finally a word of consolation and encouragement. But today he would not start in, Goldschmied had made up his mind to that. The stubborn *mof*, thought van Tuinhout, he knows damn well I won't ask him for money. I can wait. After the third dozen Our Fathers Goldschmied had enough. To hell with him, he'll never be as generous as me.

All right, Goldschmied broke the silence, how's the homework going? Van Tuinhout was overjoyed. He still had the rabbits to feed and the supper to prepare. Perfect. He got the best mark in everything. How do you do it? Why, it's at least forty years since you went to school. I don't understand a word of it. Neither does Kees. Not even the teachers, if you ask me. You must be a genius. Every single answer was right. To tell the truth, the work is much too hard. He's only twelve. Yes, I know he's lazy. Maybe not lazy, but neglected. It's always that way without a mother. I can't keep after him all day long. And he takes advantage. It's lucky we have curfew at eight, or he wouldn't get home until morning. You should see the friends he bums around with all day. A bunch of thugs. Juvenile delinquents the whole lot of them. Every day I expect him to be locked up for theft or murder. He's capable of anything these days. In the street? The kind of people you find in the streets these days. Riffraff, soldiers, and whores. Respectable people don't go out. Don't exaggerate, said Goldschmied in whom this subject (streets, going out) touched a sore point. Look here, Meneer Goldschmied, war breeds criminals – what they see now they imitate later. Wait and see what happens after the war (I should live so

long, thought Goldschmied). And said aloud: I should live
so long, Mr van Tuinhout.

What do you mean, Mr Goldschmied, you think I'm
telling fairy tales? What do you know? Sitting night and day
in this hole. Have you any idea what's going on outside?

Have I any idea what's going on outside? asked Goldschmied with a slight shake of his head. (Why are the goyim
so dumb? After all, I'm a Christian myself, so it can't be the
religion: Goldschmied's everlasting puzzle.) That's it, Mr
Goldschmied. You just sit here. Sometimes I envy you.
Would you like to change places, van Tuinhout? I didn't
mean it that way – but it's hard. Every day new regulations,
sometimes you don't know if you're still allowed to use the
pavement, because some of the regulations aren't posted.
People vanish into thin air for no reason at all. Yes, you can
consider yourself fortunate, Meneer Goldschmied, you're
out of the rain at least.

So it's raining too?

Van Tuinhout looked at him with suspicion. With Jews
you can talk, with Protestants you can talk (he himself was a
member of THE BRETHREN OF THE BLESSED VIRGIN,) but with a
Christian Jew, a Jewish Christian, you don't know where
you are. The Christians are hypocrites, most of all the
Protestants, the Jews are too smart. To be on the safe side, he
took Goldschmied's question literally.

This morning the weather was good, he said, but it may
very well rain tonight. Get on with it, said Goldschmied
impatiently, he couldn't stand it any more.

As I was saying, Kees is getting to be more of a gangster
every day. Do you know what he did yesterday? He took the
ferry across the Ij and found himself a girl, a child, maybe ten
years old . . .

Nu? (Goldschmied was growing more and more
impatient.) He's only a kid himself – you want him to sleep

with an old woman?

Believe it or not, Meneer Goldschmied, he really did sleep with the child, but the police caught him in the act. I'll be surprised if they don't put him in jail.

He is a little young, Goldschmied admitted. At his age I was apprenticed already. Sixteen hours a day. We supplied umbrellas all the way to Budapest. No, for such things I didn't have time.

That's what I've been telling you, you're living here like in a hothouse, so sheltered. You can be glad you haven't any children.

Glad, no. Except maybe right now. Children, that's all I need.

Anyway, Meneer Goldschmied, everything is getting more expensive and the money is worthless.

That was the cue. Goldschmied took out his wallet and gave him the hundred guilders rent he was going to give him anyway. But van Tuinhout had certain principles. And one of them was: You can't ask these poor persecuted people for money. Renting rooms was his profession, hiding people was patriotism. If his protégé wished to contribute something of his own free will, he couldn't refuse. But never in all the world would he have asked.

Bring me the next batch of homework soon, said Goldschmied, or the boy will be left behind.

Just one question. Doesn't the teacher notice that his homework is right and his answers in class wrong?

The teachers these days, Mr Goldschmied, aren't teachers: they're students who've flunked their exams. Today you could be a professor at the university.

I ask you, Goldschmied shook his head. Is it such an honour to be a professor at a university? My umbrellas are more interesting and it's a better living. But if the war keeps on much longer and the homework keeps coming, I'll be

163

ruined. After the war, I'll need a flood to put me back on my feet.

Meneer Goldschmied, I'd like you to do me a favour.

What? You're asking me a favour?

The gentleman who's coming today, van der Waal his name is, he doesn't know you're paying me one hundred guilders a week. If it's all the same to you, please don't tell him. I have my reasons.

Don't worry, Mr van Tuinhout. I'll be silent like a tomb. I don't think I'll speak to him anyway. I'll just ignore him.

You promise, Meneer Goldschmied.

I promise. All day I'll look at the wall and pretend he's not there. You can rely on me. You have your reasons and I don't even want to know them. But now you must excuse me, I'm busy.

Between ten and twelve. All right?

A few minutes more or less don't matter, van Tuinhout, and in case you decide to put him somewhere else, it'll be all right with me too. I can manage for money, but the air here is another matter. I could do a good business in air if I had some, it's fantastic.

The knock came at about half past ten. Goldschmied looked up from his book. There he is. Exactly between ten and twelve. You can trust van Tuinhout. Van der Waal, said Goldschmied to himself, that means either Birnbaum or Wollmann. But he was mistaken. The young man who crawled in, Goldschmied guessed him to be nineteen, was called Weintraub.

To err is human. Weintraub had red cheeks, sweaty hands, and short-cropped hair. He had big blue eyes, a fleshy nose (poor boy, the bone is missing, thought Goldschmied) that looked Jewish at the end, but only at the end. He was short and thick-set. Had on a blue sweater and corduroy trousers, introduced himself as van der Waal, and

164

tossed his small suitcase deftly under the bed.

Van Tuinhout showed his face for another two minutes in the opening, darting glances intended to impress it once again upon Goldschmied that the matter of the hundred guilders was a private arrangement between van Tuinhout and Goldschmied.

Goldschmied bent down to van Tuinhout and whispered: 'Don't worry. We practically won't see each other.'

Van Tuinhout handed him two copybooks. These are for next week. I'll bring the other two tomorrow.

Goldschmied took the copybooks and put them too under the bed. The wall was closed and the two sat on the bed.

Goldschmied looked the young man up and down, decided the view was incomplete, and said: Stand up. Weintraub stood up. Goldschmied got up too and stood beside him.

'Good. You get the shorter blanket.'

Maybe the young man was shy, he said nothing and looked the other way. How do you like it here, Goldschmied interrupted. Isn't it cosy?

Weintraub, his first name was Egon, saw the one chair, the bookshelf over the bed, the calendar of the Swiss Alpine Club with the pencil hanging from a nail, and at the foot end of the bed (he couldn't believe his eyes) a cross a foot high with a crucified Jesus on it. He couldn't take his eyes off it.

That, Mr van der Waal, is mine. So are the calendar and the pencil. But the blankets belong to the landlord. No talking in here except in a whisper, even if it wrecks your voice, and don't breathe too much either. Air is very important, we've got to economize. What you exhale I inhale and vice versa, so I hope your teeth are good.

Still not a word out of Weintraub. He just looked at Goldschmied.

Goldschmied had sagging cheeks, a bald head, an enor-

165

mous nose, and a chin that receded like a flight of steps. His lips were two thin lines, drawn down at the ends. Weintraub put his age at sixty. Actually he was only fifty-two. His hands were large and broad, he had sunken shoulders and a paunch. Two fingers of his right hand, pointer and middle finger, seemed to be crooked. Reminders of a wound in the First War.

With these fingers, said Goldschmied, I swore allegiance to Franz Josef; God punished me by making them crooked. My name, by the way, is Hubertus Alphons Brederode of Utrecht, but you can call me Efraim Goldschmied, that's what I call myself to show sympathy for the Jews.

Otherwise I'm a Christian, a real Christian, as you probably noticed right away.

(Still no sign of life from Weintraub.) A Christian, see, a goy, not one of us, one of them. Now do you see what I mean?

But baptized?

Thank God, you can talk. I was beginning to think they had cut your tongue out. Yes, baptized. Disgusting, isn't it?

Weintraub shrugged his shoulders. It's a question of taste. But are you hiding as a Jew or as a Christian?

Ha, a khokhem yet. Both, my young friend. This isn't only the cave of the Maccabees, it's also the catacombs of Amsterdam. I'm hiding double, so to speak. You see, I'm not an ordinary baptized Jew, I'm a convinced and pious Christian. I'd have had tsores either way.

Either way? Why as a Christian?

Some day I'll tell you the story of my life, but there's no hurry, because I will have the honour of seeing you again. But in a nutshell: I am the deacon of a congregation in the Nederlandsche Gereformeerde Kerk. You know the church on the Overtoom, the Church of Saints Peter and Paul? Well, I, Goldschmied, am the deacon. Yes, the Catholic name is misleading, a leftover from before the Reformation – after

166

the war we'll change it with God's help. And you, Weintraub? You're a Jew, I hope. Because two goyim in here would be too much. And I wouldn't be able to convert you.

Nobody can convert me. I'm not interested in such things. I'm of Polish origin.

Polish? Goldschmied could hardly contain himself. He almost shouted. Polish – don't say another word. Jescze Polska niezginela. He nearly fell on Weintraub's neck.

But, said Weintraub, I was only a baby when I came to Holland.

Doesn't mean a thing. Once a Pole always a Pole. What luck!

What's so lucky, you want to know? It's not so quick to explain. Polish isn't just a nationality. It's not so simple. The Poles are the chosen people the Jews would have liked to be. And why davke the Poles? Because the Poles have what the Jews haven't got. Sense and faith.

The Jews have no sense and faith? You're joking.

Pan Weitraub, I ask you, if the Jews had sense would they have gone on being Jews? Not a chance. They would have gone over to the new religion long ago. And because they have no true faith, they are the worst heathen in the world in my opinion. Absolutely.

But, Mr Goldschmied, Weintraub protested . . .

Don't interrupt me just because I'm right, that's how it is . . . They're always talking about God, but they don't really believe in anything, except money. Sure, they are good at making up ethical laws in God's name, for everything they've got a law, but what's all this got to do with religion? Nothing. The whole Jewish religion is full of practical advice, but the sense of mystery, the feeling for holiness, that they haven't got; just like the Germans and that's not the only reason.

The Germans? What are you talking about?

Goldschmied didn't like to be interrupted. You want to know what I'm talking about? Listen and you'll find out. Why do the Germans shout so loud about nation and blood? Because they're not a united nation. It's exactly the same with the Jews; they shout too loud about their Jehovah and His chosen people. There's something fishy about that. So you'll ask what's fishy? Well, I'll tell you: their religion, that's where it begins. That's where everything begins. Between you and me, Weintraub, the Jewish religion is no good. What do I mean, religion? And what do I mean no good? I'll tell you, and Goldschmied whispered mysteriously: Because Jews have no religion and because they stopped being a nation thousands of years ago, that's why they have such a lousy time.

Moralizing, that's what they do. Philosophizing. The Greeks, the Romans and the English, they got somewhere in this world – except as individuals, the Jews never accomplished a thing, not where it counts, and what counts is to find a union between man's need of faith and his individual humanity. The Jews are still what they always were, scattered tribes of merchants and Bedouins with a small group of intellectuals, from a little, insignificant Mediterranean country. Super-chauvinists, all their national feeling is nothing but primitive clannishness – like the Indians. And their racial purity? Racism, my dear Weintraub, was invented by the Jews, not the Germans. Azoi it is. And only azoi.

Goldschmied leaned back against the wall, exhausted but happy. Come to think of it, thought Goldschmied, a fool is better to talk to than a wall.

Weintraub was a kind of Palestine pioneer – a quarter Zionist, a quarter orthodox Jew (by upbringing), and the other half Dutchman. Until driven underground, that was two years before, he had worked on a farm as a hired hand. He had graduated from secondary school, though very late.

Illness had delayed everything in his short life. He had been tubercular since the age of thirteen. Work and fresh air on the farm had done him good – the coughing fits had stopped; and he had been lucky during his two years in hiding, always somewhere in the country – his last hiding place had been raided, someone had denounced him, he had escaped at the last moment. Van Tuinhout's hideout was only temporary; the friends in the underground who were helping him were well aware that a consumptive in a wall was a danger to everybody.

A temporary solution, for a week or two at the most, until they could find him a new hideout with a peasant or gardener.

He had expected it to be small, but not this small; he had expected a bed of his own. How could he share a bed with this old codger when he didn't share a single one of his opinions?

But his ups and downs had made Weintraub philosophical. Well, he said to himself, it's an experience. I only hope he's not homosexual. That I couldn't stand.

Goldschmied was not homosexual – sex seemed never even to occur to him. Sex is not for me, he would say, it's for women and children. What interests me is my business, making umbrellas, and theology. Everything else is playing around.

They lived through the night, each rolled in his blanket, back to back (twice Weintraub woke up because he thought he was going to suffocate, but somehow he survived) until the grey dawn trickled in through a pipe connected with the chimney. When Weintraub sat up and rubbed the sleep from his eyes, Goldschmied was already sitting on the other side of the bed, his back turned to him, an open book on his knees and muttering something. He swayed his body, fell into a soft sing-song – reminding Weintraub in every way of his father chanting his morning prayers.

Goldschmied prayed in Dutch and Latin – both with the same Yiddish accent, crossed himself three times at the end, kissed the book, and put it back with the others above the bed.

Of course you don't pray. You heathen – now come the exercises, then comes breakfast, such a breakfast you won't get in Krasnopolsky – everything here is home-made – even the scrambled eggs. Stand as thin as possible against the wall – good. And now, one, two, three, four – Goldschmied lay down on the bed, propped up his back and began to bicycle in the air. After five minutes he said: That's for the legs. Now for the arms. He thrust his hands out to both sides a dozen times, each time hitting Weintraub in the stomach. (You hippopotamus, can't you make yourself thinner?) In conclusion a few knee bends.

That's that, said Goldschmied, it's healthier than tennis, and it doesn't make you perspire so much. Now it's your turn. Goldschmied stood on the chair and beat time.

One, two, three, four, one, two, three, four. And so on. That's enough. Save the rest for tomorrow.

At nine van Tuinhout brought in a basin of water.

Mr van Tuinhout, the young man has to have his own water. We're not married. Goldschmied handed him the urinal to empty. He needs his own bottle too. What you Dutchmen need is a little of our Polish tidiness.

Goldschmied washed from head to foot, showing thin white legs, a blubbery back, and sunken buttocks.

Van Tuinhout came back five minutes later with Goldschmied's breakfast, a large cup of black coffee sweetened with saccharine, two slices of bread and margarine, and a dark-yellow mush on the edge of the plate – fried egg-powder.

He took away the basin and brought it back five minutes

later with fresh water. Weintraub, who had decided to spend three days at a public bath after the war, dipped a corner of his towel and rubbed his face with it. Goldschmied looked up: Oh no, my friend, that won't do. After all, we sleep together. You wash yourself properly from top to bottom, or you can move to a hotel.

Weintraub mustered him. The hell with him, he thought. Not even my father had the nerve to tell me to wash and where.

But as a newcomer, he could only give in to the elderly goy.

Breakfast was cleared away, the bed made, and they sat on the bed, Weintraub with his legs crossed, Goldschmied with his elbows on his knees and the book on his chair.

Three weeks later. Weintraub was still there. I predicted it, Mr van Tuinhout, in six months he'll still be here – with God's help we'll move to the old people's home together. Van Tuinhout had nothing but curses for the situation. The underground had hoodwinked him. As it turned out, Weintraub was penniless. What should I do, Mr Goldschmied? I can't put him out in the street. He can't pay. What should I do?

I'll make you a proposition, Meneer van Tuinhout. Just forget about the few cents he would have paid you. Put it on my bill. Give me twice as much homework.

Now what does he want? Van Tuinhout sucked his teeth. Does he think he can pull my leg?

I'll speak to my aunt – she has money, I can't ask persecuted people for money. I'll speak to my aunt, that's the best way.

Are you sure?

My aunt is obligated to us. My wife took care of her when she was down with varicose veins. She's got to help. She has more money than you and Weintraub put together.

Weintraub, said Goldschmied, we've known each other

now for three weeks – and it looks like we'll be together for ever. To tell you the truth, I've almost got used to it; it's been like a change of air. But now, seriously, if you want to be my friend, you've got to stop coughing like that. That cough will cost us our lives. Coughing is all right in peacetime – you should have done all your coughing before, because now it can cost us our necks. Weintraub flushed. I thought, he said, it had stopped. But now it's started again. I doubt if I have six months to live. Six months, Weintraub, six months is a long time.

Yes, but the end can come any day. I never told you, Mr Goldschmied, but now I've got to tell you. I have tuberculosis. I can die any day. Goldschmied looked at his new friend sharply. If you're telling me the truth I won't be so hard on you any more. A man marked by death deserves consideration, special consideration. Marked by death? What does that mean in times like these? Weintraub couldn't stand it. What do you think will happen to you if you stick your head out of the door? Marked by death. It sounds so tragic – actually I may live to be seventy. But you, Goldschmied, how long do you expect to live – without tuberculosis?

Goldschmied didn't like the way this conversation was going. He was willing to feel sorry for a poor sick man, but that the candidate for death should predict an early end for him, Goldschmied, that was too much.

Weintraub, said Goldschmied – he wanted to get this thing settled once and for all. I'm not afraid, you see I'm living in the grace of our Lord Jesus Christ. My Jesus loves me, He'll see me through, His mercy is great, His will be done, as it says in our prayer. We'll see.

Now, after three weeks, Weintraub had ceased to live in a dream. The wall had become reality; actually he was very happy to be with this fellow Goldschmied.

172

He was ashamed of his coughing. Coughing was a sickness and he was ashamed of being sick. At the approach of a coughing fit – Goldschmied had learned to recognize the signs – he wrapped his young friend's head in a blanket, which he removed ten minutes later.

Every day there were three or four fits and the previous night had been especially bad. Something's got to be done about you, Weintraub. Maybe I should keep watch at night.

Weintraub didn't know what to say. Yesterday he had spat blood again. He felt the cough tearing his lungs to pieces, he was simply spitting them out. That cough is deplorable, disgraceful. What could be done?

Van Tuinhout is bound to turn up with good news any day. He's got to get out of this wall – if he doesn't, he'll die and everybody will be in danger. What day is it? he asked.

Goldschmied scrutinized Weintraub. He took the calendar (peasants ploughing a field. The Alpine Club's motto: He who sows will reap). Your twenty-fourth day, Weintraub. It's my two hundred and eighth. You don't catch up with me. This is the last winter. Next year you'll be in Jerusalem and I in my church. One more winter, Pan Weintraub. What's one winter? I'm too old for skiing anyway. I'll stay here.

Knocking. Goldschmied pushed the hooks aside. Van Tuinhout appeared in the opening; a stranger was with him. One after another, they crawled in.

The stranger was large and broad-shouldered, with protuberant cheekbones and a wide chin. He wore glasses and a cap.

He looked like a repair man from the telephone company. This is Verhulst, van Tuinhout introduced him. He knows a peasant in Frisia who'll put van der Waal up.

But it won't be cheap, understand, said Verhulst. Goldschmied understood. How much is not cheap?

Fifteen hundred guilders. We're not getting anything from the underground.

Fifteen hundred guilders. That's a lot of money. Van der Waal hasn't got any. The underground is broke too. So what will we do?

Yes, what will we do? Hasn't he somebody he can borrow from? asked Verhulst.

Have you somebody, van der Waal? Goldschmied looked at him sternly. My parents are gone, said Weintraub. I have relatives, but where they are I don't know. I'll make you a proposition. I'll give you a pledge. He looked through his suitcase and brought out a small tin wrapped in paper. The three looked on eagerly. A pocket watch came to light.

It had a modern dial and was chrome-plated.

It's worth three guilders, said Weintraub and looked from one to the other. He was ashamed of his childish treasure. But it's worth a million to me. After the war I'll give you fifteen hundred guilders for it. It means a great deal to me.

Verhulst looked at him under his glasses. Goldschmied looked away. Van Tuinhout played with his false teeth. A short silence.

Weintraub put the watch back in its box, wrapped it in the same paper and replaced the rubber band around it. He put it in his suitcase and shoved the suitcase under the bed.

Goldschmied was first to speak. In this wallet – he took the wallet from his jacket – there's still a hundred guilders. The last. Until my committee sends me some more money, that's all. He handed van Tuinhout the wallet. Van Tuinhout turned it over twice, thought of opening it to have a look, because he couldn't believe his ears, and decided to let well enough alone. He put the wallet down beside Goldschmied. Verhulst gave him a glance.

Van Tuinhout stood up, followed by Verhulst, they opened the trap, and Verhulst climbed out first. For a few seconds van Tuinhout's head remained in the opening. He gave Goldschmied a look of reproach and astonishment. My aunt won't do it, Meneer Goldschmied. She can't right now.

Goldschmied reached under the bed and gave van Tuinhout two copybooks: Here is the homework, Meneer van Tuinhout. The last. The trap closed. They were alone.

Weintraub, it's hopeless. You can see that. No money no life. I can't keep myself any longer and you're done for too. Weintraub – Goldschmied looked at him out of eyes in which this world was already extinguished – Weintraub, my friend, I think it's all over.

Weintraub's voice had a nervous flutter and seemed to come from far away: I won't survive it, neither here nor in Poland, Mr Goldschmied, but you, no children and baptized, all you have to do is get yourself sterilized, and you're free.

Goldschmied's whole body swayed and he spoke louder than usual: Jesus suffered more, and that's why He understands. He's got to help, because no one else will. He, the Anointed One, is the only God. How do we know? Do you know the Talmud?

Why so serious, Goldschmied? You forgotten how to laugh? What kind of laughter, young man, did I ever have? Goldschmied continued:

He and He alone is the Anointed One; it is written in your holy Talmud, but one has to know how to read it:

When a man stands up and the others remain seated, does it mean that those who remain seated, as I am seated here, are inferior to the one who stands up? Or does the one who stands up wish to dissociate himself from those who are seated? People stand up for various reasons. For instance, to mention only three: a man stands up because he has something to say and wishes to be seen; or he stands up because he wants to see something that he can't see when he is seated (for instance, if I want to see what is written on the Cross – as it happens I know it by heart – I have to stand up), or he stands up simply because he doesn't want to sit down any more.

In the first case – he wants to speak and be seen, in other words, he wishes to exalt his spirit, but to exalt one's spirit means to come closer to the Holy One, may He be praised. This standing up is therefore a good work.

In the second case, however – when a man stands up because he wants to see what he can't see sitting down – it means that his soul thirsts for wisdom, for wisdom does not come down to a man who is seated.

Therefore this standing up is also good.

And now to the third case – if a man stands up because he doesn't wish to be seated any longer, he is likewise doing a good work, for the heart in which dwells the love of the Almighty, holy is His name, is filled with joy and jubilation and wishes to be seated no longer. To sit, is it not to mourn? Therefore it is good to stand up: but what does this mean?

It means that the spirit, the soul, and the heart lift themselves out of their abasement, and standing up is to sitting as life is to death. When Rabbi Gershon ben Yehuda asked his student Rabbi Naphtali: Why do some stand up while others remain seated? he was really asking: How is it that some rise up from the dead and others do not? What does this mean? It means above all one thing: Some can rise up from the dead and others cannot. So you see, Rabbi Gershon admits (would he otherwise have asked such a question?) that there is such a thing as standing up, or resurrection, from the dead. But who can rise from the dead before he is judged? Who doesn't have to wait until the Prophet Eliyahu announces the Messiah? Who? Only someone who doesn't have to wait for the Messiah. But if someone can stand up from the dead without waiting for the

Messiah, can he be an ordinary man? Not in the least. Can he be an extraordinary man? No, because an extraordinary man is still a man. Therefore he must be what no one else can be, namely, the Messiah Himself. Therefore He who has stood up from the dead is the Anointed One. His name is Jesus Christ. Who else?

As a baptized Jew without children, Mr Goldschmied, you'd only have to be sterilized and you'll be a Messiah yourself. You'll be able to stand up as much as you please – even in the tram, in the train, anywhere. And when you go to the cinema, you can take standing room.

Young man, Goldschmied gave him a friendly tug on the ear, you are making fun of me. But sterilization is no joke.

Take it from me, Mr Goldschmied, if they'd let me. This very minute. But they won't let me. They need me the way I am, half dead. But you? Goldschmied, who had grown fond of his young Polish friend, looked at him with a fatherly tenderness. They don't exactly need you, and aren't you being a little frivolous, van der Waal? Tuberculosis isn't enough for you, you want to be sterilized too?

Anything, Mr Goldschmied, anything is better than to die before your time. Even if they left me nothing but a mouth and a lung, believe me . . .

Goldschmied wagged his head: Yes, I admit, in your case breathing is the most important thing in life, and maybe if I had your . . . maybe if I, myself, well, you know what I mean – maybe I'd talk the same as you. But as it is? Am I a mad dog? Weintraub, who had come to love Goldschmied like his own uncle, was dismayed. The moment Verhulst disappeared through the trap, he saw himself getting out of the train at Westerbork. Westerbork, stopover on the way to the end. This has been going on for two years and twenty-four days. The Germans aren't to blame, or the Nazis, or the Verhulsts; it's this disease that's come down in my family.

177

He died of TB, they'll say, nobody has him on his conscience, they'll say. Nobody will have me on his conscience, said Weintraub aloud, he died of TB, they'll say. A lump rose in Weintraub's throat.

But Weintraub, Goldschmied laid a hand on his shoulder, what do you care what they're going to say? Who dies for his obituary? Do you really think this world still needs more examples of murdered innocents? There's no shortage. No one will miss you except a few friends and relatives. Sad, but that's how it is.

Although Weintraub had his eyes on Goldschmied's lips as he was saying these words, his thoughts were far away: It's all an accident, pure chance that there was no other place that week; chance that I had to fall in with this van Tuinhout, who has to make his little deals. The fifteen hundred guilders wouldn't have done me any good either, or would they? The J is the meat hook. Everybody has to carry his own – if you've got it, they gas you right away, if you haven't they kick you and torture you until you admit you've got the hook. And then they hang you up on it.

It's not the J that matters, even without it you can be sentenced to death, it's the admission that counts. Admit you're a Jew. If it comes to that, what will Goldschmied do with his Jesus and his Talmud? He can live. He has only to say the word. He's not a Jew. He doesn't want children. He doesn't bother with sex, or not very much. Has he a martyr complex? Why does he want to die when he can live? If they find him here, that's an admission in itself. They'll smash the Cross over his head. As deacon of a Christian congregation, he had no need to hide.

He looked at Goldschmied, who was passing a finger over the mountain ranges on his calendar, and tried to read his thoughts.

The word sterilization had but one effect on Goldschmied,

178

to throw him into utter confusion.

The possibility of saving his life was more than his nerves could stand. How could he explain this to Weintraub? But he had to explain (or Weintraub would die with mistaken ideas and false hopes). The essential difference is between killing and being killed. Murderers after their deed need human mercy – but the murdered need divine mercy in advance. Goldschmied also knew it was all over, not with life, that would be no problem, but with hiding. Two hundred and eight is a cabalistic magic number, if you could only discover its meaning. Goldschmied knew the Talmud, Rashi's commentaries, and of course his Old Testament (how he had time left for his umbrellas was a mystery to his closest friends); when he wanted to start on the Cabala, it was impossible to find either teachers or books.

How easy it is to miscount, Weintraub. The years were too short. Two hundred and eight is a mysterious number. Why just two hundred and eight? Is two hundred and twenty better, or two hundred and fifty? The highest number is the best, but is there such a thing as the highest number? There is only infinity. But I've taken out my insurance on that. Is there any better life-insurance, with lower premiums, than Christ? If there were, Weintraub, wouldn't I have taken it out? A Jew who takes up Christianity has lost nothing and gained everything. For good Christians such a Jew is a Christian, but for anti-Semites I'm still a Jew. So I turn anti-Semite; that way I can go on seeing myself as a Jew (between you and me, I was an anti-Semite before and as a Jewish anti-Semite I couldn't stand myself). So now you know why I turned Christian. It makes everything so simple. With one exception: the regulation about the childless baptized. On one rotten condition they let me live – as a Jew, no conditions, they just kill me. They let me choose something I wouldn't wish on a dog. You have no choice. You don't have to turn into a dog; you can die like a normal, healthy human being.

That's why I don't want the day to come, because tomorrow I'll have to make up my mind and I can't choose. Because if a normal, healthy human being lets himself be killed when he has a choice – is that normal and healthy? And I'll tell you what's sick about the Jews: their religion. As Christians or Mohammedans they could have trampled on the world and established the Jewish justice they're always raving about. But no, they didn't want to. They didn't have the imagination or the power; to succeed they'd have had to become Christians. But they didn't feel like it. Instead of martyring, they let themselves be martyred; looking on is impossible. For Jews. Now I'll tell you the truth. I didn't hide because I'm a Jew, I hid to avoid choosing.

Then you can stand and look on, Mr Goldschmied: Weintraub was furious at the Talmudic complications with which Goldschmied tried to talk himself out of his fear. Why won't he admit it? The Nazis are to blame that a man like Goldschmied has to think such thoughts. By hair-splitting he had turned their guilt into a guilt of his own.

Jewish conceit, Mr Goldschmied; you won't even let the other fellow keep his guilt. How can anybody know where he stands if the victims take the guilt for themselves? No wonder they all climb into the trains of their own free will; they think it serves them right, and not that they're wronged.

Maybe we all of us suffer injustice, but does it really matter, Weintraub? If tomorrow I decide to be sterilized, I can look on as they finish you off.

The Nazis would have fired their ovens in any case, believe me, if not with Jews, then with Poles, Russians, gipsies. If they had let the Jews, God forbid, look on, or even worse, if they had let them help make the fire, not one, Weintraub, but the majority would have gone over to the

Nazis. When it comes to anti-Semitism and organization, the Nazis could learn plenty from some Jews. But how could such a thing have been justified in the eyes of God?

Mr Goldschmied, you talk like that because you're scared stiff.

I talk the way I do because tomorrow you'll lose your life and I my sanity. To tell you the truth, I've considered it from time to time – but for the last three weeks, since you came, my last chance is gone too.

Do you love me as much as that? asked Weintraub bewildered.

Like my own flesh.

Just admit you're a Jew, Goldschmied, and we'll go together.

What's that, Weintraub? You know I am a pious Christian. My mazel!

Frankly, Mr Goldschmied, I have no sympathy for you. I'd rather be a live onlooker than a dead victim. You talk and talk. Religion, holiness, the Jews' mission. All a lot of phrases, slogans. Choice, dog, guilt. I don't give a shit about all that. In a few days they'll strangle me and burn me like a leper, and that's the end of Sholem Weintraub. They'll give me a number on a mass grave, coloured with gold dust, and I'll never, never be alive again. Resurrection is nothing but Talmudic hair-splitting, mystery, smoke and sulphur, hocus-pocus, theological speculation. There is no second time, not before and not after the Messiah, and He doesn't exist anyway. I want to live, Mr Goldschmied, I want to live and breathe and I don't care how – like a dog or a frog or a bedbug, it's all the same to me. I want to live and breathe, to live.

Weintraub's face turned dark-red and his glands swelled. Goldschmied reached for the blanket and threw it over Weintraub's head. But Weintraub shook it off. His eyes glittered, sweat stood out on his forehead, and his hands trembled as he shouted: Live, breathe, I want to live, live. Goldschmied flung himself on Weintraub, and tried to put his hand over his mouth, but Weintraub flailed like a wild beast and went on shouting. Live, live, I don't want to die like a dog. Cut off my balls and my cock with it, cut off my hands and feet, but let me live and breathe!

Weintraub broke into a coughing fit, and he spat and wheezed blood. Goldschmied sat stiff and pale on the chair and watched his young friend Weintraub who was beginning to decompose even before he was dead. Goldschmied's eyes stared into the void. There was a knocking and drumming on all four walls. Shouts were heard and a car stopping. Weintraub flailed about on the bed and seemed to choke with coughing. The drumming grew louder, angrier.

Goldschmied stood up, climbed on the chair, and tore the Cross off the wall.

Shouts and stamping feet were heard, followed by unexpected silence, then boots pounded through the corridor, the trap was pushed up with rifle butts, and a voice under a helmet shouted: Come on out, or I'll take the lead out of your ass.

An ambulance, Goldschmied heard himself saying from far off, he wants to live, but he's going to die on us.

Goldschmied crawled out first, he stood with upraised hands, the Cross protruding from his coat pocket, waiting for them to bring out Weintraub.

Two of them reached through the opening and picked Weintraub off the bed like a sack. Goldschmied was unobserved for a moment: running isn't in my line, he decided.

In the living-room stood two more men in uniform, through the window a small crowd and a patrol car could be seen. Van Tuinhout sat there with bowed head, staring into space.

The policeman with the most stripes was in Dutch uniform. He turned to Goldschmied.

You can take your things, of course, or just wait here and I'll get them. The first to come down was Weintraub, looking pale and sick – escorted by a policeman. Then came the Dutchman and his German colleague.

Each carried a small suitcase. I'll take them to the car, gentlemen, your friend seems unwell.

He carried the suitcases to the car. Yes, Meneer, said the Dutchman, it's disgusting work, but what can you do. I'm only doing my duty. I have a wife and three children. One of my sons is just about your age, he said to Weintraub. Just lie down on the bench and if we drive too fast for you, please knock and we'll slow down a bit. There's no hurry. Goldschmied had recovered from his terror and Weintraub too felt new-born in the fresh air, even though it was damp and cold. So you know what it's like to feel sick? he asked the Dutchman.

I know plenty. O.K., he said to the German driver, but not too fast. The Dutchman turned round to Goldschmied: I've been suffering from headaches for years and this work is driving me crazy. I've got a good recipe for headache, Inspector, you should try it some time, said Goldschmied. Sugar water, bring it to a quick boil, mix it with honey and melted butter, and drink it down while it's still hot.

You don't say? And it helps? I'll have to tell my wife about that, she'll make me some up tomorrow. We menfolks are lost when it comes to cooking and such. Am I right? Ha-ha-ha.

Yes, that's a good idea, the German driver put in. I'll have to try it. I'm crazy about sweet things. Chocolate, candy, and all that kind of stuff, that's for me. I used to work in a chocolate factory, that was a few years back, it belonged to a Jew, but not any more. I should have known you then, called one of the policemen in the rear, a ramrod of a man in his forties. I'm crazy about chocolate myself. A nice piece of chocolate, as I always say, is as good as a meal. You can keep your chocolate, said the second policeman, who was standing with his rifle beside van Tuinhout. What I like best is fresh dill pickles and marinated herring. Naw, sweets ain't for me.

Why argue, Goldschmied interrupted. It's all a matter of taste. One likes sweet, another likes sour.

That's the truth, the Dutchman agreed. How's your friend? he asked Goldschmied. I hope he's feeling better.

Weintraub listened to the whole conversation with closed eyes – chocolate, dill pickles, sugar water with honey – they're talking about normal things. In the last three weeks the conversation was all about religion and Jews and guilt. I almost died in that hole. If Goldschmied hadn't got me so riled with his high-flown speeches, maybe we'd still be sitting in that hell.

Suddenly life seemed to him reasonable and simple again, and he was ashamed of having acted like a madman. Now that there was air to breathe, all his fear had left him. The air has done you good, said Goldschmied, glad to see Weintraub looking normal again. Get a good lungful. You never know when there'll be more.

Van Tuinhout, who had so far sat silent and motionless, turned to the Dutch police officer: Who's going to take care of my boy when I'm gone?

The state, I suppose, I don't know exactly how it works – but the Germans always look after the younger generation, you've got to hand it to them.

They were taken to Gestapo headquarters. Don't be afraid, said Goldschmied to the livid Weintraub next day as he was carried from the cell to a waiting ambulance, we'll meet again, I'll take bets on it.

184

Weintraub didn't have one word to say for himself – his case was clear. After a lengthy cross-examination Goldschmied's case was also settled, and a week after his arrest he too arrived at the transit camp. No sooner had he passed through the gate than he ran into his friend, looking healthy and cheerful. They hugged each other. There were tears of joy in Weintraub's eyes. I can breathe again, Goldschmied, he cried with joy, what do you say to that, I can breathe again.

Well, said Goldschmied, the air here isn't bad (it was a warm autumn day and the children were playing in the sun), it's nice in the outside world. You look new-born.

You look much better too, Goldschmied. Why, you stand up straight as a soldier. I always thought you had a hump.

Yes, Weintraub, if they just leave you alone, if they just let you stand and sit and walk up and down . . . it's like a second life.

I've missed you, Weintraub. When are you leaving?

Weintraub said blandly: My train leaves today. At five o'clock.

Today? When I've just come? Can't you take a later train? What's the hurry?

Today, Mr Goldschmied. Today at five. We shall meet again.

Still in this world?

Why, naturally, in this world, Mr Goldschmied, do you really believe those stories about Poland? Now that I'm feeling better, I don't believe them any more. Sick people get such crazy fears.

Goldschmied looked at Weintraub for a long moment, then turned and left him. As he left he said: You're right, Weintraub, we've got to keep our health, with all this fear we might as well be dead. Keep healthy, have a good trip, and make sure you get there all right. We shall meet again.

A week after this conversation the two did indeed meet. Weintraub was climbing the steep stairs to his holy Jerusalem and Goldschmied to his Jesus on the Cross. For to tell the truth, the city of Jerusalem is not so very big.